FILTHY LIAR

AINSLEY BOOTH

WWW.AINSLEYBOOTH.COM

ABOUT THIS BOOK

Jason:
It's been a long, lonely five years. I never stopped caring for Ellie, even after I realized she'd conned her way into our firm in order to get a scoop. Now that she's back in my life, we have a lot to catch up on—even as the world burns around us, I'm going to find a way to prove she can trust me.

Melinda:
I'm not his Ellie. I never was. She doesn't exist, and if Jason starts digging into Melinda the journalist, that won't end well for me, either. But now that some of our cards are on the table, maybe I can use Jason one last time. For the greater good.

ALSO IN THIS SERIES:

Hate F*@k (Cole and Hailey)
Booty Call (Scott and Ali)
Dirty Love (Wilson and Tabitha)
Wicked Sin (Taylor and Luke)

www.ainsleybooth.com

This series started out as two distinct things: a huge, sweeping saga about geo-political issues, stretching out over many books, and at the same time, each book is an individual, deeply intimate story of two messy people finding each other in the chaos.

Filthy Liar continues that tradition. This book starts in a more ripped-from-the-headlines way than I first envisioned, jumping over the end of this series as I originally planned it. If you're here for the messy love part, that's very much the same as I always planned it to be, don't worry.

I really wish that billionaire rapists were properly held to account in the real world, and on the page, but maybe what we need now is for them just to be dead in both places. So, RIP* Gerome Lively, you horrible monster.

As a reminder, I started writing this series in 2014. It's not my fault shit got real. All similarities to real events or people is purely coincidental.

A detailed content warning is available on my website.

~ Ainsley Booth

* The P does not stand for peace, I promise.

[1]

MELINDA

WHAT DOES justice really look like? Not a billionaire's suicide, that's for sure.

Somehow I always knew the journey would end like this. Not in a court of law, not at the end of the imperfect course of justice being served, but cut short by an act of brutal selfishness.

Of course Gerome Lively killed himself. He was in jail, denied bail, and looking at multiple life sentences with no chance of ever seeing freedom again. Removing himself from the justice process was his final "fuck you" to every woman who came forward about him abusing them when they were girls.

After everything the survivors of his sex-trafficking did to bring him to justice—twice, because the billionaire had a disturbing number of friends in high places who didn't care what he did, or worse, had been a part of his depravity—he took the coward's way out.

I get the news alert on my phone. A minute later, my college roommate texts me.

Caroline: The fucking coward.

Melinda: My thoughts exactly.

Caroline: The conspiracy theorists are going to love this, too.

Melinda: Not if we can help it.

Caroline: You need to come back to D.C. so we can have drinks.

Caroline is a federal prosecutor. She didn't work on his case, and we've always been careful about work boundaries. When I wrote my book about Lively, the one that thrust him back into the public eye and triggered a new investigation, we had an ethical firewall from the moment I decided to cover the story on the off chance it might blow up in her jurisdiction.

But it wouldn't be out of the realm of possibility for her to be a source on one of my stories. I open the sliding door and step out onto the deck. It's still early on the west coast and the Pacific Ocean is a beast this morning. Far below, waves crash against rock.

Go back to D.C.?

It's the last place in the world I want to spend any time. But to see Caroline—and maybe for a story, if there's something she can only tell me in person—I'll get on a plane.

After booking a flight, I go to social media to see what trends are being pushed around Lively's death. I know even before I go to Twitter there will be chatter that he didn't actually commit suicide.

I'm not wrong. And there's just as much chatter about who might want to "silence" him, as if there was ever a chance in hell of him turning on his acquaintances. As if Lively's celebrity "friends" had anything to fear from him, as if the dubiously elected POTUS had a need to silence him. Or my favorite: as if the British prince who spent his mid-life crisis "accidentally" being a pedophile had somehow ordered a hit to happen at Riker's Island.

All of those rumors assume a lot more competence in certain high places than actually exists.

But most of all, they deny the depths to which a depraved criminal can sink.

Gerome Lively never valued anything beyond twisted power. Stripped of it in almost every way, he used the last tool in his disposal to cause pain one more time.

For five years, I've been writing about this story, and others like it. For five years, I've worked within the bounds of the law. I'm a journalist and freedom of the press gives me some latitude to hold sources in confidence, to investigate stories.

Lively's suicide means a lot of information is never going to come out in court.

He didn't die to protect anyone's secrets but his own, but that doesn't mean there wasn't collateral damage.

I put my phone down and stare out at the ocean. I need to clear my mind and remind myself of the endgame.

No more secrets. For anyone.

[2]

JASON

The text arrives while I'm glad-handing at a glitzy reception at the French embassy.

Cole: New client. Meet at the office in an hour.

I set my glass on a tray carried by a passing waiter and head for the door. I'm done here, anyway. Every so often I get lucky, because here's the thing: big decisions are made in backroom deals, yeah, but sometimes those back rooms are actually the corner of a party. Power brokers huddled in plain sight.

Not tonight, though. It's not a complete bust. Halfway across the room, I catch the tail end of a discreet conversation that I file away. If I'm free tomorrow night, I might be able to make an appearance at the Kennedy Center tomorrow and make a new friend.

A lot of my job is knowing the right—or wrong—person

t the right time. I keep my eyes and ears open and take nothing at face value. Everyone is lying, to themselves or others, and when I can use what I know to get what I want, it's a beautiful thing.

A beautiful, twisted, broken thing, but that's my life.

The how and why of what I do as a crisis management specialist—a fixer, one of Washington's best—that's not important. What matters is that I get results.

Thanks to a generous tip, the valet staff have my car close at hand. I slide behind the wheel, and as soon as the door is closed, I hit play on the audio file waiting on my phone. It's the start of a dossier, read in a cool, electronic voice programmed by Wilson Carter, our resident hacker.

Our client, it turns out, is Jeff Mayfair.

Billionaire, philanthropist, and the older brother of a former SEAL buddy who has done some work with us— Scott Mayfair, who married Cole Parker's youngest sister-in-law.

Fucking hell.

"Mr. Mayfair has no criminal charges in his background, either domestically or according to Interpol. He is a dual citizen of the United States and the United Kingdom. He has extensive holdings in both countries, recently divested from the parent company, Mayfair Enterprises..."

There's nothing in the dossier that is a surprise to me. There's also nothing there to hint at what his reasons for hiring The Horus Group might be, either.

By the time I pull into the parking garage beneath our building, I know one thing for sure. Our client has almost certainly been lying, somewhere and for some reason, and now it's come back to bite him in the ass.

This is why my firm exists—to get the rich and powerful out of the trouble they should have avoided in the first place.

But we're all human. I don't judge anyone, as long as they pay their bill promptly.

Upstairs, I find Cole waiting in the boardroom with Jeff. Wilson is on one of the screens on the wall, video conferencing in from his home in some secret location in the Pacific Northwest.

Our fourth partner, Tag Browning, arrives just as we're doing introductions. Seven years ago, Tag was a disillusioned DC cop going through a divorce. I used that to my advantage and laid the facts on the table for him. We were going to make a real difference in the world.

Nights like this, I sometimes wonder if we've done enough in that regard.

"Jeff, this is Jason Evans, our president," Cole starts.

"We've met in passing," I say. "I'm a big fan of your brothers." In addition to Scott, they have another brother who is a pilot in Air Force.

"As am I." Jeff sighs. "If any of this touches them, I'll be damn sorry."

"Why don't you start by telling us what this is?" Tag gives him a big, disarming grin. It's an act, and one he's very good at.

"I'm being blackmailed."

Ah, that old chestnut. None of us look surprised. I take

a seat at the table—not the head, but one of the seats along the side.

Cole sets our standard non-disclosure agreement in front of our new client. "Tell us everything. Whatever you leave out will be the nail in your coffin."

"There are photos of me with girls—underage girls—on Gerome Lively's plane." Jeff pauses as Cole loses his calm mask.

Well, no fucking shit my partner is unimpressed. Lively kidnapped his wife. But none of us are on Team Defend Predators.

"I'm sorry," I say with all the chill in my voice. "We don't work on that kind of case."

But Jeff doesn't move. He doesn't get mad, he just keeps going. "The photos aren't real," he says levelly. "And I can prove it."

"So what's the problem?"

"The proof is classified. I'm willing to risk sharing it with you behind that NDA, but I can't make it public. Not without risking jail time and losing contracts worth billions of dollars that would put my employees out of work."

A quick glance at the screen on the wall tells me Wilson is already digging.

Silence bounces around the room.

Cole doesn't say a word. Tag glances his way, then to me. Finally, he looks up at Wilson, who gives a tight nod. *Go ahead. I haven't found anything—yet.* Tag leans back in his chair, sliding into the good cop role with ease. "Look, Jeff. Can I call you Jeff?"

The billionaire nods.

"The thing is, as you say, proof can be faked just as easily as photos. Maybe—*maybe*—you can survive pictures, if there's nothing else. Literally, nothing else can come out like this. And don't get me wrong, I know we're all men with urges here, but—"

"I don't like younger women," Mayfair interrupts. "I *definitely* don't like girls. That's disgusting. Lively was disgusting, and not only is that photo not real, but I went out of my way to never cross paths with him. That's not the kind of business person I am. Period. You won't find anything."

"What do you like, then?" Tag shrugs. "Bondage? Threeways? A little good-humored humiliation?"

Mayfair's throat bobs.

Tag grins, another broad we're-all-guys-here friendly face. "Is that it? You're afraid something else gets out?"

"I wish it were that simple." Mayfair scrubs a hand over his face, then sighs. "I've never had a particularly long relationship, and while I like the physical side of it as much as the average person, I'm not into ropes and whips and chains—in either direction."

When he doesn't continue, Wilson looks up to the camera, making eye contact from the other side of the continent. "But you do make all of your intimate partners sign NDAs."

Jeff nods. Then he gestures to the form document we had presented to him, with our own signatures on it. "It was presented to me as a good idea by our legal team, a long time ago, and no partner ever had an issue with it. But the photos I'm being blackmailed with...they have a copy of that NDA. It's been forged with a young woman's name. I have never met her in my life. I swear to you, that's the truth."

I stand up and pace to the sideboard, where someone—Cole, probably—filled a pitcher of water before the meeting started.

Once upon a time, we had a receptionist who made sure there were bagels or muffins there as well, but then I fucked her for a summer. And she took off for the hills.

So I'm not really one to judge another man for fucking up his life in the most ordinary of ways. I pour myself a glass of water. "Tell us about the blackmail. How long have they been in contact with you, what have you paid them already, and how did the contact begin?"

Without hesitation, he digs into the whole story. He hasn't yet paid anything out. They made contact to his personal email address, not through an intermediary, and he's been slow-rolling them with his responses for three days.

"Why did you come to us? Why not handle this with your internal security team, or with Scott?"

Jeff shakes his head. "I'd prefer my brother not be involved. He's living his best life in California, and he's been through enough." He glances at Cole. "I came to you instead of my own team because I'm not sure it's not an inside job. I know Scott trusts you, and if I went to him first, he'd probably say I should hire The Horus Group."

"Well, our reputation stands for itself. We'll do our best to help you," Cole says, the first time he's spoken since we sat down. His brow is still pulled tight, but the storm clouds have passed. It's as close to an endorsement of this client as we'll get.

I nod, then look at Tag, who turns to Wilson on the screen.

Our hacker jerks his chin up. "On it."

———

The next night, following that hunch I had based on an overheard conversation, I make sure the wrong people see me buy a pretty young socialite a drink at the Kennedy Center.

By the end of the concert, she's warned about me. *He's dangerous. The rumors are true. Jason Evans may look like a Washington insider now, but he's an ex-SEAL who isn't afraid to get his hands dirty, and his first clients were...well, Amelia Dashford Reid is dead now, isn't she? He got her husband off a murder charge, you know. But that family...*

Fuck those fuckers. That family—at least the younger generation—has removed themselves from the narrative, and the ghost gossip doesn't matter. I'm not above using it, though.

Over the next week, a few things slide into focus.

First, we don't think Jeff Mayfair is the only person being blackmailed with false documentation of connections with Lively. So far we haven't found anyone else willing to dmit it, but the routing number for the off-shore bank ccount has pinged around a bit on the Dark Web in recent months.

They're a hired gun, and hired guns like regular work.

Instead of paying them off, Wilson had Mayfair make a low-key but public statement waiving all NDA agreements, personal and professional. It sparks speculation that Mayfair might be running for public office, and still the photos don't make a peep anywhere—and the blackmailer doesn't return with new demands.

The second thing that pings onto our radar is that my half-brother, Mack, has started a quiet and unexpected campaign to join the president's administration. It's an attempt to course-correct from the inside, and it's an uncharacteristically bad move, but he's the older brother, the more successful brother, and guidance between us has always moved in a single direction. He gave us the seed money to start The Horus Group. We've outgrown the need for him as a silent investor, but that history still exists.

And the third and final element on the three-dimensional chess board for our firm is the growing public acknowledgment that the current administration has lost the trust of its closest NATO allies. It's been a long two years with an incompetent casino king position as the leader of the free world, and global relations are getting frayed at the edges. This is my area of particular interest. It's why I was at the French Embassy. It's why I'm concerned about Mack's agenda.

I've narrowed my target to three vectors of interest. The

French Ambassador, the principal secretary to the Prime Minister of Canada, and the newly exiled Belarusian opposition leader. Tracking their movements over the next week will show me the path that the world's power brokers are setting us upon.

Which brings me back to the socialite.

A week after our drink at the Kennedy Center, I make sure she bumps into me at her favorite coffee shop, and now tonight—just like that, because pretty young socialites love danger and a warning is better than an endorsement—I'm a fill-in at her Friday night dinner party because someone else got food poisoning at the last second.

On the one hand, it's not ethical to deliberately make someone sick. On the other, the loser I bumped off her guest list is a fucking asshole and I won't lose sleep if he spends the night turning himself inside out into his toilet bowl while I listen to the tipsy ramblings of the French Ambassador's very young wife—who just happens to be the socialite's best friend.

That's the plan, anyway.

But plans tend to go out the window when the rubber hits the road.

Also, I'm getting too fucking old for this.

Seven years ago, I lived for this shit, good or bad. It was all the same to me, a jaded ex-special forces operator who had lost his moral compass somewhere on a mountaintop in Afghanistan. I found it again a few years later. Well, it wasn't mine, exactly. I've had to borrow one from Cole, who managed to re-grow his personal ethics when he fell in love in the most unlikely of places: right in the middle of the snake den.

Hailey Dashford Reid was the thorn in our side, the problem child who refused to play along as we—The Horus Group, Washington's highest paid fixers—tried to rehabilitate her parents' reputation. Cole fell head-over-heels for her, and now Hailey is also Mrs. Parker.

She remains a bit of a thorn in my side to this day, but it turns out she was right to refuse, and us cutting ties with a certain set meant we weren't overly exposed when Amelia —her snake of a mother—was toppled.

Few people know that's what happened, but then few people know anything about the truth of Amelia Dashford Reid's life, her bizarre family relationships, her attachment to Gerome Lively, and the strings she was pulling in the most exclusive halls of power.

I don't even know if I have the complete picture myself.

What I do know is that change is upon us. Seismic shifts on a geo-political level, and when the rumbling finally stops, everything will be radically different.

I intend to be standing on the rubble when it's over. Everything that happened in the past is done, over. All that matters is what comes next, and who benefits from it.

But first, I have a dinner party to infiltrate. The French Ambassador is in my sights. Or rather, to start, his pretty young wife.

———

"Jason was a Navy SEAL, you know." The hostess drops her hand to my forearm and squeeze. I flex against her touch and she giggles.

If I wanted to fuck her bareback tonight, I could. Jesus Christ, this was like taking candy from a baby.

And her friend, the ambassador's wife, is no different. As soon as our hostess moves on to the next cluster of people, Camille leans in. "The special forces? The ones who catch all the bad guys?" Her smile widens. "We have such men in France as well, but we don't make movies about them."

From behind me, I hear a small snort of laughter, but when I turn my head to the side, I can't see where it came from.

"That's what I like the most about the French," I murmur. "Your discretion."

"I'm very discreet." Her tongue slides daintily across the inner edge of the corner of her mouth. A subtle, non-verbal invitation. "You know, I have free time every so often. When my husband travels for work."

Candy. From. A. Baby. "Any chance you might be free next weekend?"

"I'll be all alone from Thursday evening until Monday."

"Not if I have anything to say about it." I wink at her and give her my card. "It was a pleasure meeting you, Camille."

"And you." She glances over her shoulder. "I should mingle, yes?"

"We both should." I make it clear that I would rather be alone with her, but social duty calls.

As I move around the pool, I wonder who overheard that conversation. It doesn't matter, really. If someone interferes, more the better. I have no intention of actually having an affair with Camille. She's not my type. Too young, too absolutely unaware of op-sec.

My goal here tonight was threefold.

First, for my own reasons, I wanted confirmation that her husband would be out of Washington for those precise dates.

Pulling my out my phone, I text Wilson the update.

Jason: The Ambassador will be at the summit.
Wilson: Acknowledged.

Second, I wanted to create the impression for all curious observers that I am actively looking to get cozy with his wife. Misdirection achieved.

My third goal was the first thing I did when I arrived—I dropped two micro drones along the back wall of the property while being given the grand tour.

I quickly check the tracker app on my phone, to see that they haven't been detected. The GPS trackers show them exactly where I left them.

Excellent.

As I put my phone away, I catch sight of a heart-shaped face from my past. Bee-stung lips, dark eyes with thick, sooty lashes. Black hair—that's new—but there's no mistaking who it is.

Ellie. She's dressed as waitstaff, in black pants and a white shirt, wearing an apron, and in the split second it takes for me to register the familiarity, she pivots and disappears inside. I dart around the pool, following the woman who ghosted me five years ago.

The woman who was once my receptionist, and then disappeared without a trace.

Heart pounding, I stop inside the main hall of the Rock Creek mansion and listen for the direction of the catering noise. Clatters lead me almost to the kitchen, but I duck into a dark powder room as I catch sight of her in the doorway.

"I'm really sorry to do this." Her voice drifts towards me. "Are you sure it's okay if I go?"

"Yeah, we're good. Thanks for your help tonight. You actually make a pretty good waiter, you know that?"

She laughs, but there's a tightness to her voice. Does she know I'm this close?

The next beat of the conversation is obscured by another clatter, then there's silence. I chance sticking my head back into the hallway, just enough to catch sight of the kitchen, but it's empty.

She's gone.

I sprint to the front door, not caring if I'm seen. She's already made me, disappeared into thin air. Again.

The gate on the far side of the circular drive is closed, but of course she didn't valet park her car.

She was here posing as the help. *The little con artist.*

"A waitress dropped this on her way out," I say to the valet approaching. Despite the growing furor inside me, my voice sounds calm. I show him my phone. "Did you see her?"

[3]

MELINDA

FUCKITY FUCK FUCK. I really wanted access to this catering gig to last a few weeks longer.

As soon as I'm around the corner of the house, I kick it into high gear and sprint through the side gate. I'm not sure I can outrun Jason, even if I'm wearing clothes more suited to a foot race than he is.

He looked good in that suit.

Truly, absolutely not what I should be concerned with right now.

I can't risk trying to cut across properties in this neighborhood. Too much money, too many connections. Guaranteed security systems that police would actually respond to alarms from. My bike is three blocks away, because there wasn't enough parking at the hoity-toity residence for guests and the hired help.

Can Jason find me in three blocks? Jesus Christ, why did I not grin and bear the discomfort of tracking him while

I'm in town? Being caught off-guard like this is completely disruptive to—well, everything. Did I not think I might run into him?

I knew I could at some point, but tonight? The chances were low. When I worked for him, the socialites were always someone else's job.

I could have handled running into Cole or Tag. I would *love* to see Wilson again. But Jason? I repeat, fuckity fuck fuck.

I need to get to the next block, then make a decision.

Left or right.

I risk a glance behind me, and I don't see him. I don't hear his footsteps, either, but those could come any second.

Which block is shorter?

Left.

The sticky summer humidity isn't making this fun. My kingdom for a breeze, holy shit. A car's engine growls to life a block away, and my pulse jacks up again. I force my breath out as steadily as possible while sprinting at top speed.

I get around the block and the tucked-away parking lot is in sight. I sprint the whole way, ignoring my protesting lungs, and don't stop until I'm on my bike and roaring towards Georgetown.

It's not that I'm afraid of Jason, exactly. I'm not afraid of anyone. But I don't have time to deal with the mistakes of the past right now. I have enough on my plate with the mistakes of the present.

It doesn't take me long to get to my new apartment

building on the edge of Georgetown, conveniently located right between the Russian Embassy and the Naval Observatory where the VP lives.

Nosy girls like to be in the middle of the action. You never know when you're going to overhear a grumpy staffer say the right/wrong thing while getting coffee.

I pull into the parking garage, quickly decelerating. A quick glance in my rearview mirrors as the secure door rolls up, then I pull through and wait until it closes behind me.

Once I stash my bike in the storage unit I got instead of a parking stall—one of the main reasons I picked this building—I head upstairs to my second-floor studio.

I don't need a lot of space. Room for a bed, a desk, and a window for my aloe vera plant. Her name is Monica, and I bought her because she reminds me of California. The sun, the salty air.

The distance between me and my past. *Jason.*

Monica—being a plant—is unfamiliar with that complicating factor. Lucky Monica.

I set my helmet on its spot next to the aloe vera, under the window that overlooks the Naval Observatory, and I go to the kitchenette to get an extra-stiff drink.

What was Jason's interest in crashing the party tonight? Because I have no doubt that's how he got there. He looked cozy with the French Ambassador's young wife, which had to be strategic on his part.

He had never been interested in playing the bull. But maybe he's changed in the last five years. It's none of my business. Whatever his business is—at least personally—I burned any claim to that man's flesh when I ghosted him and his firm.

But politically...maybe there's a story there.

I wrinkle my nose. I don't like the idea of Jason As a Story. It's why I left. But that was in the before times. Before the last election, before everything changed, before Lively killed himself. Before Amelia Dashford Reid went off the deep end.

And now I live in an empty studio apartment while I try to hack the time-intensive process of finding sources in a city I've done my damnedest to ignore for half a decade. Hence the catering job that I can't go back. Fucking Jason, what a party-pooper.

I snicker to myself and toss back half my drink. He'd have liked it if I called him that. He'd find it cheeky.

The tequila burns, so I set the glass down and fire up my computer to check my encrypted email addresses. A few messages from sources for long-game stories I'm working on back burners, one weird lead idea that doesn't sound like it will go anywhere—yes, all the rich old men in this town are pedophiles, almost certainly, but I'm not going to fall for a variation on the pizzagate story. I run a trace and sure enough, that email address has been used by a semi-infamous loser asshole who will do anything to make women look bad.

Delete.

The final note in my inbox makes me sit up a little

straighter. It's from an account inside the DC police force, and I recognize the name. Detective Kendra Browning. Ex-wife of Tag Browning, one of Jason's partners in The Horus Group. What are the odds?

I'm not the type to believe in coincidences. My skepticism has driven me to sometimes find patterns and stories where none exist. Early in my career, that was drummed out of me. I had to learn that sometimes, a coincidence is just that.

But still...

I flip over to Twitter. Does Detective Browning have an account? Not that I can tell. I do, albeit an anonymous one.

There aren't many people in this world who know anything about me. There are no photographs of me as Melinda Gray, Intrepid Girl Reporter. Anonymous author of *Private Jet, Private Hell*. I have social media accounts and by-lines, but they're all dead ends as far as finding a real person behind them. So the chances that Detective Browning knows that I know her through a different channel are slim.

My pulse thumps heavy at the base of my throat as I read the subject line for a second time.

From: Detective Kendra Browning
To: Melinda Gray
Subject: Request for an interview
(background information)

I click into the message.

In the course of an investigation, some of your articles have popped onto my radar...

I scan the rest of the message and type a standard reply.

From: Melinda Gray
To: Detective Kendra Browning
Subject: Re: Request for an interview (background information)

I never reveal my sources. I don't think I can be of any help to the police in this matter.

But I don't hit send. I read her message back again, then scowl at the blinking cursor. I drain my glass, go to the kitchen for a refill, then come back.

The cursor flashes at me as if to say, *this isn't the right reply*.

Why not?

What am I missing? What is my instinct pinging on, and why can't I *see* it? I dig out my burner phone, the one with only one contact—Caroline—and fire off a cryptic message. Then I close the laptop. I don't need to reply right away.

Maybe it's that I don't want to reply without disclosing that we know each other from another time, another life. I can picture the good detective from her visits to the Horus Group offices.

I could disclose that prior connection, if need be, but not in writing. I have before, to Taylor Dashford Reid, a former client of The Horus Group and a fellow absconder to the west coast. In the year since I printed her story, I've never had any reason to think she told anyone who I am. But a third brush with that past life, and on the same night as a near run-in with Jason?

It's enough to make an already paranoid investigator think something was definitely up.

A glow of headlights out my window catches my eye. A slow-moving caravan of vehicles is driving down one of the lanes on the property of the Naval Observatory. There's a story there, in the comings and goings of the property's most famous residents—and the visitors they get.

D.C. is full of stories, though, and I don't know if I want to tell them anymore.

Maybe my next project will be my swan song in journalism, and I can silently fade into the night. I'll reinvent myself as a barista in Kansas or something similarly wholesome.

Maybe one day I'll even find someone to share all of this with.

I can't imagine how that would even go. *Funny story...*

Laughing to myself, I reach for my glass—but I freeze before I pick it up. Why on God's green acres did those two words pop into my head like that? Jason Fucking Evans.

"Funny story..." is how we ended up crossing the line between employer and employee in the first place.

[4]
JASON

I **SHOULD CLOSE** my door and leave her alone.

Alone.

That's precisely the problem.

Cole is on vacation—fucking his beautiful girlfriend on a beach in Hawaii, I'm sure—and Tag and Wilson are doing a security system walk-through with a client in Arlington.

Which means Ellie and I are all alone in the office, and any second, I'm going to get up from my desk and go find her. I'll invent a problem. Ask if there's coffee—which there isn't, because I'll have already dumped the pot on the way to reception.

She'll get up and lead the way, her pert, round ass bobbing in front of me like a matador's red cape.

Which makes me the bull.

Fuck, yes.

Except...no.

For one thing, it would make me a hypocrite. And for another, I'm pretty sure that if I give in to my base need for her, this isn't going to end well.

I'm not the upstanding SEAL I once was, for many reasons, not the least of which is that I covet my employee's ass.

And her tits.

And her soft, wet mouth.

A knock at the door interrupts my fantasy and I snap my shit tight. "Yep," I say coolly, clipped.

Ellie marches efficiently up to and around my desk, leaning her hip against the side of it. "There are six schedule conflicts on your calendar next week. I've flagged them all in bright red so you can go in and fix them."

I swear under my breath. "Again?"

"Your work load has changed. It might be time to hire an assistant."

I can't do that. "I'll think about it. And thank you for flagging the conflicts. That's not your job. I appreciate the quick eye."

"No problem." She hands me a neatly written message. "Also, the young Miss Conroy has called twice this afternoon looking for an appointment."

I make a face. I fucking hate socialites. "We should hire someone to hire the nuisance cases."

"She's harmless."

Exactly. I don't have time for harmless. I'm rather busy

with the exceedingly harmful types. "Do you want to take the appointment?"

She blinks in surprise. "Me?"

"If she's harmless...why not let her think you're the crisis specialist?"

Ellie's cheeks turn pink. "I dunno. I'm not...I wouldn't know what to do."

"You're very capable." My voice runs rough, and I clear my throat. I hold the note back out, but she doesn't take it, so I stand, which means I'm suddenly looming over her. When I push the paper into her hand, her fingers wrap around mine, and a sizzle of electricity burns my skin.

She looks up at me and her lips part, her eyes wide.

Fuck.

I don't move.

She does, though. She ducks her head and twists, breaking the connection. I take a hard step back. *Lock that shit down, Evans.*

I can't hit on my employee.

I won't.

She wiggles the piece of paper in the air as she heads for the door. "I'll handle her."

"Charge her a full consultation fee."

"I'm going to have a woman-to-woman conversation with her and convince her how to solve her problem without hiring G.I. Joe," Ellie retorts.

This is safer ground. I snap back at her. "We don't do pro bono work."

She stops in the doorway and looks back at me, her gaze piercing. "We do when it's a good cause."

"Socialites are rarely good causes."

"An excellent point." She spins around and leans her shoulder against the door frame. "Hey. funny story..."

She trails off as she realizes my gaze is locked on her legs. The swing of her skirt has settled back around her knees now, but as she spun, I caught the unmistakable sight of old-fashioned stockings hooked to a garter belt.

Silence falls between us.

I'm supposed to prompt her here. Ask her what the funny story is.

I don't say anything.

She holds my gaze, and my cock thickens beneath my desk. "It's almost lunch," she says huskily. "Should I order something in?"

———

An hour later, takeout containers litter my desk and my jacket and tie have been discarded. Ellie is sprawled in the chair across from mine, her skirt carefully covering those stockings I caught a glimpse of, and she's doing some healthy damage to the chicken adobo.

"Have you thought more about handling the Conroy inquiry?"

She wrinkles her nose at me. "It's not my job."

"It could be."

"I like what I do. I don't know if I want to take on more work." She frowns. "Unless you're not happy with—"

"God no. You're the best thing that's ever happened to this firm."

"Thanks." She gives me a soft smile, almost sad. "It's a point of pride, I guess."

I think I've stepped in something here and I should back the hell up. I sit up straighter. "You're very good at it. You manage our different personalities well."

"You're as close as brothers. I don't need to manage much. You're...really a family."

I'm surprised that she seems surprised. "You weren't expecting that."

She shakes her head, then leans forward to swap the chicken for the BBQ pork. "Nope."

"What did you expect?"

Leaning back in her chair, she re-crosses her legs, and her skirt climbs up her thighs a couple of inches. "Ego clashes."

"We have those sometimes." My jaw twitches.

"But you're the alpha."

Damn fucking straight. "Sure."

"Does that ever get old?" She blinks, and now she's looking at me—really looking at me—and I'm blindsided. So much for her being soft and me stepping all over her feelings.

Sometimes I wonder if it's Ellie who's the secret alpha. "No," I say carefully. "I knew what I was signing up for.

We need to project a certain strength and it has to be authentic."

She nods, accepting that answer.

But her next question is just as sharp. "Do you ever think about cutting loose?"

"Never."

"Is that your military training?"

"Sure."

She giggles. *Giggles*, which isn't a sound I've ever heard from her before. Ellie laughs, sometimes with us, sometimes at us, and always with the confidence of someone who sees us as the boys we are. This laugh is different. It's a private laugh, just between us, and it might be an act, it might be sexual, but I don't care.

I mirror her nonchalance and lean back in my own chair. "Do *you* ever think about cutting loose?"

"Never," she whispers, mimicking my word and my voice at the same time.

Ah. A game.

I grin. "Military training?"

"Sure." The word slides between us like a silk sheet dropping from her body.

Ellie doesn't have a shred of military training in her body. It's one of the reasons we hired her. She's an innocent-but-smart girl from the Midwest. New to D.C. and untainted by the corruption outside these walls.

"If we were to cut loose, what would we do?"

"The two of us?" One of her eyebrows curves high. "That's an intriguing thought, Mr. Evans."

I groan. It's quiet, but we're all alone and she's not that far from me. Just on the other side of my desk.

Her lips part, and she crosses her legs the other way again. "Is it okay if I call you that?"

Jesus. "Ellie—" I cut myself off. My dick is rock hard in my pants and my brain is swimming, but I'm not stupid. "We can't—"

"Of course not." She smiles lazily. "And so we won't. This isn't happening."

She looks like a very satisfied cat who has caught a canary, and as far as I'm aware, I'm no fucking bird. "Can we speak frankly?"

Her lips twitch. "Is that not what we've been doing?"

I stand. I need to pace. I need to think, to be sure of what I say next. Because this is so wrong, so absolutely off-limits unacceptable that if I proposition her, it'll be like threading a needle. I'll get one chance to do it perfectly, or it'll be all fucked up.

I roll my sleeves up as I move past her to the window. The left first, neatly to my elbow. Then the right.

"We're all alone," she says from behind me.

I don't turn around. "I won't take advantage of you."

"You aren't."

"I'm your boss."

"I absolve you of that role for the afternoon."

"Is that what you want?" I turn now, and she's standing in front of me. "One afternoon?"

A dark shadow passes through her gaze, then she blinks, her dark lashes brushing her cheek. When she looks at me again, it's gone. "I want a lot of things I can't have," she murmurs. "Do you have to be one of them?"

Fuck the rules. I haul her against me and her lips part, a tiny gasp rushing between us before my mouth consumes hers.

She softens immediately in my arms. Her fingers wrap around the back of my neck, crawl up into my hair, and the curvy front of her body somehow finds a perfect fit against the hard angles of mine.

As I kiss her, I back her up. Taste by taste, step by step, until we're at my desk.

Then I lift her and sit that perfect ass on the smooth wood surface.

"I want to see those stockings," I rasp. I drop my hands to her silk-clad thighs.

She spreads her legs. "Be my guest."

Gliding my hands over her muscles, I feel the lace and the ribbon straps first. Then I pause, playing my fingertips over the bare skin at the top of the stockings, before lifting my hand and easing her skirt up her legs.

She wiggles to help, and my right hand drops between her thighs.

Bare skin, warm and inviting, is even better than perving on stockings. I give up on my plan to only have a good look and give in to my craven need to touch her. I get more than I could ever have hoped for. "Ellie, you aren't wearing any panties."

"I lost them," she says breathily, and not really at all innocently.

A heady thrill charges through me. "When did you... lose them?"

"After lunch was delivered."

I groan and stroked her flesh again. "Fuck, you're already wet."

Her breath hitches, and her sweet little pussy gets even slicker against my fingers.

"You needed this, didn't you?" I graze my teeth on her earlobe, the dirty talk turning me on just as much as her. "Were your thighs aching as you sat across for me?"

"Yes," she gasps.

I nudge her legs wider. Her pussy lips open and that slippery goodness spills onto my palm. This is messy on every level. Physically, emotionally, professionally. Knowing that I shouldn't be playing with her on my desk, that this is not the place and our receptionist is not the person for my depraved desires only turns me on further.

When I turned around and she was standing in front of me, something deep inside me unlocked. I won't stop unless she stomps on the brakes. I'm going to make all the mistakes right now and love every one of them.

"Let me see you." I growl it out, a hoarse command. "Lean back and put those legs on my shoulders."

Her eyes go wide, but she follows my instruction—and then does one better. She rocks back on her wrists and lifts one leg up to my shoulder, but the other she curves out wide, bracing her thigh against the edge of my desk. "Don't stop touching me," she whispers. "It feels so good."

That makes me feel like a God damn giant. Fuck. I nod as I hold her gaze, then slowly look down. Her legs are spread lewdly around my body, her tan thighs an open invitation that leads right to a private swatch of creamy white skin, with a swollen pink cunt right in the middle. Waxed bare and glistening everywhere my fingers drag her juices. Up and around each outer lip, over the inner folds, and back up to a dark pink clit that hardens a little more with each pass.

My fingers look obscene against her delicate sex. Like I'm violating her, and I am. This is wrong, so wrong, but now I've touched her and we can't un-ring that bell.

She bucks against me as I circle her tight little entrance with a blunt, thick fingertip. I need to see my cock there, need to watch as her body stretches to accommodate my dick.

I add a second finger and slide my thumb against her clit. With each rude thrust, she grinds a little harder, and when I pause, she tells me she wants more.

"Yes," she breathes. "Jason, yes. Fuck me with your fingers. Make me ride them."

Holy shit, Ellie has a dirty mouth. "Aren't you a sexy little fiend," I growl. "Does this feel good?"

"So good."

"It looks good. You're fucking beautiful, you know that?"

"Yeah?" She bites her lip as I work my fingers in and out of her.

"Can you come like this?"

"Oh...yes..." Shuddering, she rocks her hips. "I'm close already. I was close as soon as you kissed me."

I won't let that go to my head. "When you come, I'm going to fuck you."

She whimpers. "Yes. Please."

"Do you want that? You want my cock inside you?"

"Jason..."

"You're so tight, Ellie."

"I want it..."

"Say it."

She bites her lip, then nods. "I want your cock," she whispers.

Fuck. Me.

I press my thumb down, holding her clit as I curve my fingers inside her pussy. I want her orgasm so fucking bad right now. I want to feel her come apart on my hand, and then I want it all over again with me buried inside her.

With a strangled gasp, she surges forward and clamps her hands on my shoulders. I feel the first grip around my fingers, then a shimmery ripple of sensation. The climax repeats itself, rings on a pond, and I stand there like an oak, feeling like that giant all over again, absorbing the aftereffects of the most gorgeous orgasm I've ever witnessed.

"Good one?" I ask as she presses her face into my neck.

"Mmm."

"I enjoyed it, too."

She giggles and wriggles off my hand.

I lift my fingers to my mouth, and she watches, gaze hooded, as I lick them off.

"Do I taste good?"

I offer her the tip of my index finger and she bites it between her teeth. Gently. Just enough to remind me that there's more to Ellie than meets the eye, maybe there always has been, and she's in charge here.

We do as much or as little as she wants.

If she's done now, that's more than fine by me.

But she's not done. Not by a long shot. She slides her tongue between my fingers, then slurps it back up between her lips in a lewd, arousing sound before making her next request. "I want you inside me."

Hell yeah. "Any chance that when you were losing your underwear, you happened to find a condom at the same time?"

"It just so happens..." She hops down and leans over to her purse, her skirt still rucked up high on her waist, and I rake my gaze over the swollen pink flesh between her thighs.

There's no way we're going to excise this chemistry that haunts us in a single afternoon. Whatever dark magic Ellie has unlocked today, I'm hooked. I drop to my knees, the request for a condom forgotten. I need more than a taste of her. I need to gorge myself on her flesh.

She shrieks and grabs for the desk. I've got her by the thighs, she's not going anywhere, but I love the throaty giggle she lets out as she tries to gain purchase and hold still for my oral attack.

"Jason, I want you—"

And she'll get me when I'm good and ready.

[5]

JASON

PRESENT DAY

(well, it's the middle of the night)

SHE'S A FUCKING WITCH. That's the only answer. She disappeared into thin air, and now she's parked rent-free in my head.

I don't even try to sleep. I go home to change into something more comfortable, punish my body with a hard workout, and then take a cold shower before heading to the office.

Wilson flew in a few days ago, to be on the ground here for the final stages in our Mayfair operation. Because he and his partner live in the Pacific Northwest now, and he spends most of his time working remotely, when he's in

D.C., he sticks to west coast times. And then works around the clock, anyway.

"It's two in the morning," I say when I stop in the doorway to his cave-like office.

"Eleven on the west coast," he says quietly, not looking away from his screens. "She's still awake."

In one corner of one of the monitors, there's video feed from his house, and I can see Tabitha Leighton, reclusive rockstar, curled up on the couch with a sleeping baby, their second child.

"Maybe when this is over, you don't need to come back for a while."

He nods in acknowledgment.

"I, uh..." My throat goes dry. Nerves. I huff a quiet breath, and that grabs Wilson's attention in a way everything else I've just said doesn't.

He pivots in his chair and gives me a piercing look. "What is it?"

I gesture at the live video feed. "I need you to find someone for me." He's good at that. Before he and Tabitha were together, he watched her from a distance. Worried over her from afar.

How many times in the last five years have I thought about asking him to do this exact thing? But I always held back, because deep down, I knew she wouldn't want me to find her.

But that was before tonight. My heart punches its way into my throat, like a furious fist. Then I say her name. "Ellie."

His eyebrows spike up and his mouth drops open. "Yeah," he says carefully. "Okay."

He doesn't ask why.

"Do you know where she is?" My head pounds. "Have you been keeping tabs on her?"

"No." He frowns. "I'd have told you if I was."

"Okay."

"What do you have?" He pulls up a dialog box on the screen, a back end to a database.

I swallow hard as he punches in her social security details, copied from our own records. "I saw her tonight. She was waitstaff at that dinner I got myself invited to."

He gestures at the screen. "Nothing pinging on her record since she worked here. No credit applications, no employment that I can find. Are you absolutely sure it was her?"

"A hundred percent. And she made me, too."

"What was the name of the catering company?"

I give him the details I noted, the name on the truck out back and the license plate, too. He runs a couple of searches. "They're a legit company, but a small firm. Let me see if I can get into their accounting... Bingo." He tabs through a few screens. "How many waitstaff did they have working tonight?"

"Five, plus the chef in the kitchen."

He scrolls down the screen. "That's one more than they usually use for an event that size. And according to this, they only logged hours for four of them."

"So she was there, but she wasn't officially on the

books." I roll my neck, letting it crack on both sides. "What the fuck is she doing?"

"Maybe she worked for cash."

"Maybe." But something feels off. "Can you run another search into her background? Go deeper this time."

When she disappeared five years ago, it had seemed obvious. I'd overstepped, taken advantage of her, and she'd ghosted me, deservedly. Wilson had told me he'd run a couple of searches to make sure she wasn't going to blindside us with a lawsuit—which I would have settled in a heartbeat.

I'd have given her anything she wanted.

But she never surfaced. And now I know, deep down, she's not who she appears. "She wasn't really there to be a waiter. Something the chef said to her just before she dodged. That she actually was helpful. I think she was there for another reason."

"That makes two of you." Wilson frowns. "You think she's a spook of some kind?"

Fuck. "I don't know. But yeah. Something like that. As soon as she made me, I knew. She's running some kind of con."

"Maybe she's..." Wilson trails off. "You know what? I'm not going to speculate. Don't do anything stupid while I dig into this, all right?"

"I'm not going to." I wouldn't know where to start looking for her.

"All right. I'll dig deeper, but I need you to focus as I change the subject. I have a shortlist of potential candidates for the PRISM council seat." He hesitates. "You're not going to like one of the names on it."

"I'm not going to like any of the names on it," I reply dryly. "Let's have it."

He taps a button on his keyboard, and five photographs and biographies pop onto the screen. One of them is an obvious candidate—the President, who is just vain enough to think he could be the leader of the free world and a participant in the shadowy organization that is intent on destroying it for profit. But we all know that despite Victor Best's billions made in Vegas, and the fact PRISM backed him with a slick data-driven campaign in the election, he's not playing on their level.

Best is not the kind of billionaire who successfully fills the gaping hole left on the council by the untimely death of Amelia Dashford Reid.

Neither are three of the other names on the list, all men of a certain age who are business leaders due more to luck than intelligence.

And then there's Jeff Mayfair.

"Fuck."

"Uh huh."

"Why is he on the list?" My voice slams through the silence in the room, a terse punch of words. "Why the fuck is—"

Wilson holds up his hands. "Don't shoot the messenger. The algorithm likes him a lot. Forty percent chance it's him. He's a dual citizen between the US and the UK. He retained the nanotechnology production facility in Leeds when he forced Mayfair Enterprises to go public, against his mother's wishes. His space program has been *spectacularly* successful. Recklessly so, some say. That kind of chaotic energy is right in line with PRSIM and you know it."

This is too close to home. "It's a red herring."

"It might not be." Wilson looks grim.

I shake my head. "I dunno. Let's let it ride for a few more days, I'll keep searching for intel. Maybe something will pop that will give your algorithm a completely different perspective. But in the meantime...let's keep this between us. If Cole asks for an update, give him..." I make a face and point at an oil executive on the screen. "That fucker will do. Let's pretend he's our presumptive target."

"Got it." Wilson's jaw flexes. "But if Mayfair came here with a sob story about being blackmailed in some attempt to re-focus our attention..."

Would Mayfair know that we're watching the empty PRISM seat that closely? Would he do it personally, instead of throwing a patsy in our path? "It doesn't make sense if he's some kind of evil genius."

Mayfair... He's not like Dashford Reid. He's not predictable, and worse, I don't see a way to set off a controlled detonation beneath him that he would even feel.

If Mayfair is about to ascend to the PRISM council, the world as we know it is about to change in ways I cannot even begin to predict.

Well, if Wilson wanted to get my mind off Ellie, he succeeded. "I'll be in my office."

I don't place the phone call right away, even though it's morning in Geneva. I stare out the window at the dark city on the other side. Tomorrow night, I have another party to attend. Another foray into the world of power and politics that I have come to despise with every fiber of my being.

There's nothing about this current mission that I like. The murky confusion, the reappearance of my onetime lover, and Scott Mayfair's brother at the heart of it all.

Something isn't right.

I cross to my desk and dial a familiar number.

[6]

MELINDA

After a long, sleepless night, I get a text reply from Caroline's burner.

555-451-1765: Coffee before work? Usual place.
555-788-2119: See you there.

We meet at a busy cafe down the street.

Even though we live just a block apart from each other, it's been hard to coordinate time for more than passing drinks. She's swamped in a case she can't talk about. Something has changed since she told me to come for a visit— and I ended up staying, surprising us both.

"You paged me on the bat signal devices," she teases when we get a table. "It must be urgent."

I start with the easier to talk about question. "Do you know Detective Kendra Browning?"

Caroline gives me a sidelong glance. "Yeah. How do you know her?"

"She emailed me last night. My writer account. She has questions about what I've written recently." I hesitate. "I know her from before, too."

Caro nods. She's the only person in the world who knows these two parts of my life. "She was married to Tag Browning."

"Yeah."

"Do you think she knows Melinda Gray is…you?"

"No?" Then I take a shaky breath and dive into the deep end. "I saw Jason last night."

Caroline's eyes bug out. I know, any normal girlfriend would have led with that. "What?"

I don't want to tell her about the moonlighting with the catering company. "At a party. I got out of there immediately, but he recognized me across the crowd."

"Well, this town isn't that big. Is it the end of the world?"

"No?" I sigh. "I'm not sure. I ran like hell. So at least on some level, I don't want to deal with him."

"Of course not. But if a story…was it a story that led you to cross paths?"

"Yeah." And by giving up that catering cover story, now my way into the Canadian Embassy party is going to be that much harder.

"Then you'll probably see him again. Next time, don't run. Remember, you didn't do anything wrong. I'm a lawyer. I'm advising you of your rights."

I laugh. "My right to ghost a man?"

"It's enshrined in our Constitution."

"I'm not sure it is."

"Which one of us went to law school?"

My retort dies on my tongue as her phone goes off.

She chews on her bottom lip. "Look, I don't want to change the subject, but—" Her phone rings again, and she glances at the screen. "Damn it. I need to get to the office. But I wanted to ask you—"

We both laugh when her phone lights up a third time.

"Later," I promise her. "Drinks this weekend."

She nods, then hurriedly gathers her stuff back together. "Coffee to go, I guess. And Mel—for my two cents, I like and trust Kendra. If she wants to talk, reach out to her. Hear her out. You don't need to say anything."

"Good plan."

I decide to take a chance on Detective Browning and send her an email before I finish my coffee. She replies within five minutes.

We agree to meet an hour later for my second coffee of the morning.

I'm waiting outside, in my finest sweatpants and a fitted tank top, when she arrives. She, on the other hand, is wearing a fitted black suit and looks like a supermodel. Not much has changed.

She slows down, gives me the once over, and I introduce myself—again. "I'm Melinda," I say. *"I'm Ellie, the new receptionist."*

She doesn't recognize me. "Kendra Browning. Thank

you for meeting with me." *"Detective Browning. I'm here to see Tag. We're not married any longer, no matter what he says."* She smiled back then. Today, her face is pulled tight. Whatever it is she wants to talk to me about, it's serious.

I take a deep breath. "Detective, I need to tell you that we've met before in another setting."

"Oh?"

"Five years ago, I worked as the receptionist at The Horus Group."

She frowns, thinking. Her keen gaze rakes my face. "Ellie?"

"One and the same. Well, not exactly." I pause. "So I took a bit of a gamble meeting you. I want you to know that I'm trusting you with my identity. I don't like to keep secrets from my sources."

"I'm not a source." She lifts her chin.

The whole exchange is cagey, but not unfriendly. We're sizing each other up, and that's okay. These are strange, unprecedented times. One can never be too careful.

"So if you are not a source, does that mean that you are hoping I can be a source for you?" I ask once we have lattes and have found a quiet bench.

She doesn't answer me directly. "What do you know about Jeff Mayfair?"

I choose my words carefully. "His space program is getting a lot of attention."

"I don't investigate that."

No, she doesn't. "You want to know if he came up in my research for *Private Jet*?"

"Yes."

"I couldn't find anything conclusive that connected him to Lively. Only some Dark Web chatter that sounded a lot like unfounded rumors."

"It's getting harder to separate fact from fiction," she says quietly.

"Have you heard of a single source of incriminating documents? A lot of them?"

A treasure trove of guilty consciences, one source called it. Hackers are circling like sharks looking for blood, but every lead has turned into a dead end.

There's a long, pregnant pause before Kendra replies quietly. "I've heard talk."

"Anything to suggest Mayfair is implicated in those documents?"

Another pause. "Off the record?"

"Yes."

"That's what I've heard."

Interesting. I take a sip of coffee and mull that over. "If I find something more concrete, will you go on the record?"

"If you find something more concrete, I'll find a way to press charges." She stands up. "And then I'll go on the record."

"I'm not a personal investigator," I remind her.

"I know that." She searches my face. "But I think we have a common goal here. You trusted me, I'll trust you not to expose me here. Or Caroline."

I nod silently, and she strides away as elegantly as she arrived.

Then I take a deep breath, pull out my phone, and start to dig into everyone's favorite space billionaire.

———

Fourteen hours and a quick eyebrow wax plus shopping trip later, I jump out of a hired town car in front of Jeff Mayfair's D.C. residence. After last week's rumors that he might be running for office, he's hosting a fundraiser tonight for the former Secretary of State—who actually *is* running, against the incumbent President for the nomination of their own party.

I had been vaguely aware of Mayfair's support for her before, but while I was at the salon this afternoon, I did a deep dive.

If he ends up being outed as another Lively, this support will absolutely backfire for her. Either he's confident in his innocence, or his ego is unchecked. Both could be true at the same time.

As I suspect, there is security at the door, checking invitations. As I hoped, some people have paper cards, but most are showing the invites on their phones. Now I just need to figure out a name that might be on the list as a backup to plan A...

I fall into step behind a slow moving group. "It's a shame Elaine couldn't join us," one says.

What are the chances Elaine can be a thirty-something in a dress with no back? I'm going to find out. Stopping to ostensibly dig my phone out of my purse, I let them get ahead, then climb the stairs to the front door.

I listen to the conversation as each guest checks in.

As the person in front of me gets the all clear to move ahead, I curse politely. "I'm so sorry," I say to the security guard, showing him the black screen of my phone. "I drained the battery watching TikToks on the car ride over. Can you believe it?"

Laughing, I lean forward, trying to see if I can spot an Elaine on his list. No such luck.

"Name?"

I ignore the question. "Do you think I could just plug my phone in here? I have a charger with me." I glance around. No plugs. Excellent. "I'll just..."

I move to slide past him.

A solid arm stops me. "Ma'am, this is a private party—"

"I know! I told you, the invite is on my phone, which is *dead*, so I just need to plug it in." *Come on, buddy, look at my tits.* But he doesn't. Damn it. "Right. Okay, look up my name. It's Elaine..."

"Elaine!" My heart sinks at the too-cheery familiar voice. Jason is never cheery. And it's a sharp kind of cheery that I absolutely recognize as furious underneath.

Of all the billionaire fundraisers, of course he had to be at this one.

He steps into view and slides his arm around my shoulders, a heavy shackle locking me in place next to his body. "She's with me." He beams at me as I tense up. "Glad you could make it, *Elaine*." He provides the security guard with a last name that apparently works, and with a dangerously reassuring squeeze on my shoulder, he ushers me inside.

He ducks his head so his mouth is right next to my ear. "Don't make a scene."

It's a silky threat, a promise that this will get so much worse if I don't play along. What's the worst that could happen in a crowded party full of business and political elite?

I know the answer to that, but we'll pretend I don't. Despite the fact I ran last night, and I've shown up right in front of him once again—God damn it—there is a very slim possibility Jason still thinks I'm the secretary who just didn't show up for work one day.

"Hey," I say casually. "Thanks. My phone—"

"Is dead, I heard." He steers me to the top of the staircase.

My heart pounds in my chest as we pause there, over-looking the party. There's only one way to play this, and it's light as air. "Small world, bumping into you twice in as many days."

His fingers tighten again on my shoulder. If I don't have bruises, I'll be lucky. *Once upon a time, I quite liked the bruises he left on my skin...*

"We didn't get a chance to talk yesterday," Jason says, his voice heavy with irony.

But I don't have any other choice. I keep brassing it out. "We don't really have anything to talk about…"

"Of course we do. It's been a long time, and you disappeared. I was worried about you." Was. Past tense. No longer worried about me, now worried about what I'm doing here.

I don't respond, because all the pieces have clicked together in my brain.

Mayfair.

Incriminating evidence.

An unexpected redirection of gossip in the press.

This party.

It all has Jason's fingerprints on it, a classic Horus Group blueprint plan to avoid a PR disaster.

My stomach clenches.

Once upon a time, I promised myself he would never be the subject of a story. It wouldn't be right. But his clients are fair game whether he likes it or not.

"What's your plan here?" He gestures at the party. A couple moves around us and descends the staircase, but Jason keeps me rooted where I am. Removed from the hustle below.

"I don't have a plan," I whisper.

"You sure about that?" He growls and pivots us both, moving me away from the party whether I like it or not.

My pulse jacks up as he opens a door and shoves me into a quiet library. So much for the safety of a crowd.

We're all alone now, for the first time in a long time, and this can't be the man I once knew. Though, to be fair,

I'm definitely not the woman he thought he once knew. Never was, which is...well, this is a mess of my own making.

As he crowds me up against the wall just inside the door, I catch the faintest whiff of his spicy sweet scent, so subtle that it's only noticeable when mere inches apart. The familiarity still slams into me like a freight train. I shove the recognition away. It doesn't matter.

Nor does it matter how good he looks, again, in a suit. I didn't appreciate the eye-candy enough when I had a right to ogle him.

Even angry, he's painfully attractive. The man eats danger for breakfast, and doesn't seem to have a soul...and yet there's a dark, captivating depth to him. I always did want more than was safe.

His face tightens as he looks me over. "I thought you might skip town after last night."

I jerk my chin up. "Oh, don't worry, I'm planning on it right after you let me go."

"Why? What are you running from this time, Ellie?"

"You."

"Am I that scary?" He looks like that pleases him, like he's happy to have me cornered in the dark.

I glance past him, taking stock of the room in a split second before blinking back in his direction. "You know you are."

He's not, though. Not to me, not now. Never had been. I brace myself for a volley of questions I cannot answer. It's too complicated, too messy, and this is not the time for it. There will never be a right time for that conversation.

"Who are you?"

"None of your business."

"You aren't an employee of the catering company."

"Am I not?"

"Not under the social security number you conned your way into my firm with, no you're not."

"Maybe the paperwork is still on someone's desk," I say dryly, hanging on to faint hope that he falls for the obvious explanation.

"You haven't done any work since you left The Horus Group." Crap. Of course he checked up on me. But if that's what he thinks he knows, he doesn't have much.

"I've been unemployed."

"For five years?" He laughs. "Give me some credit."

"I'm talking to you, aren't I? That's your credit given."

He doesn't point out that I'm caged against the wall by a man who easily has sixty pounds on me. We both know I'm not having this conversation entirely willingly. "Why did you run last night?"

That trips me up, but only for a second. "Oh, come on. I saw an ex-lover who I didn't want to see ever again? And yet, despite my best efforts to evade you, here you are. Imprisoning me."

His jaw flexes hard. "Ellie, we need to talk."

I roll my eyes. "We do not. I'm back in town and I would rather not see you again—"

"I know you're a hacker."

Well, that is an unexpected statement. Also, wrong. I

laugh, giddy with relief, because he just showed his hand. "You know that, do you?"

"There's no good reason for you to be play-acting as wait staff at that party. And then to show up here, dressed like that, eager to get inside these walls..." He moves in close again, this time so close I can feel the ghost impression of his mouth against mine. Five years should have been long enough to forget the scent of a man, the weight of his body, the taste of his lips...it should be, but it's not. "I don't know who you really are or what your game is, but I'm here to warn you off. You don't know what you're dealing with."

"Sounds like a threat."

"Not from me. Is that what you think? That I might hurt you?"

I shiver as he lifts his hand, and he freezes, his touch just barely grazing my cheek.

"You weren't expecting that." He grimaces as I shake my head. "Ah, Ellie." He rubs his thumb against the corner of my mouth. "I never stopped caring. It's been a long, lonely five years. We have a lot to catch up on."

Well, fuck me. That's going to make the disappearing act I do next super fucking awkward.

Can't be helped, though.

Because I'm not his Ellie. I never was. She doesn't exist, and if Jason starts digging into Melinda the journalist, that won't end well for me, either. "Not here," I whisper. "Tomorrow. Or later tonight. We can talk, I promise."

He laughs and drops his hand, but just for a second. "You'll run again." He steps to the side, curving his fingers around the back of my upper arm like they're a steel manacle. "You don't like it here? I can leave. Let's go back to my place."

I dig in my heels, dropping my weight just enough to test the strength of his grip. "I don't want to make a scene, but I will if I have to."

He tightens his hold. "Ellie—"

"I'm not a hacker," I whisper fiercely. "I'm a journalist."

[7]
JASON

I STEP BACK, shock and a bizarre sense of betrayal roiling through me. "You're a what?"

Ellie smiles, her glossy, bubble-gum pink lips curving with convincing sincerity. She never wore that color before. I don't like it, an instinctive dislike that makes no sense and really has no bearing on anything. It's her mouth, she can slick it up however she likes.

But I remember those lips stained red, wrapped around my cock. Stained red and parted as I slid my fingers into her mouth to get them slick. To work us both up for what I would do next.

In every fantasy I've had in the time she was gone, her mouth was stained red.

Maybe the bubble-gum pink is as much a disguise as the red once was. Maybe the real Ellie doesn't wear anything on her mouth at all, and fuck me for thinking about anything other than the task at hand.

Answers. I need answers.

"A member of the press," she says levelly. "And we can keep this off the record, if you'd like."

"Everything is off the record," I growl. "Every fucking thing."

"Sure." She has the audacity to shrug, and I want to punch the wall.

Instead, I pace into the middle of the library. My mind is racing. If she's not a hacker, and she wasn't tagging one of the guests last night, then what was she doing at that party? And more importantly, why is she in my client's home now? I pivot and point at her. "What story are you working?"

She's unfazed. "I'll show you mine if you show me yours. What are you covering up for Mayfair?"

No. No, no, fucking hell no.

She waits, her eyes bright.

I don't like the extra-dark hair, either.

I don't like anything about this new Ellie or her rude return to my life. But instead of answering her, I rake my gaze down her body. She's still built for sin, and five years is not long enough to erase the memory of her body on top of mine, her thighs straddling my hips. I need to remember that despite our history, she's investigating my client. Sin can't play here.

I set my jaw and prowl back toward her, stopping just out of touching range. *I want to touch her all over.* It's a dark, unbidden thought, primitive and stupid. I don't want to touch her, not really. She's lied to me at every turn. "Tell me what story you're working, first."

"That's not how show and tell works, I'm afraid. I asked, you answer."

"So you think you have a story on Mayfair." I lean in. I can't help it. She smells the same as she always did. "You're wrong."

"Then it was great catching up, Jason. I'll see you around." She moves, and I grab her wrist. Not hard. Just enough to stop her. Her attention drops to where my fingers manacle her wrist. She sneers. "What happened to you? I thought you'd turned into one of the good guys."

"There are no good guys."

Pain slices across her face, just for a second. Fuck me. I drop her arm.

She shrugs it off. "No, I get it. From your perspective, there's nothing to be done about the state of the world. Not when you come to a *thing* like this and see people who swear to the world that they are on opposite sides of every-thing hob-knobbing over a fresh oyster bar, am I right?"

I like the way she says *thing* like the word is three-week-old rotten garbage. She's not wrong.

Her voice drops to pure silk. "Spend too much time in this town and it will ruin you."

That's my line. I said it to her a few weeks after we hired her—after we hired a sweet, innocent young woman from the Midwest, I correct myself.

That woman, who I knew as Ellie, was too fucking pure for this world.

Now I don't know who I have in front of me. I doubt she's too pure for anything. But she might be too fucking smart for this world, and I need her to get wise to the reality of the danger around her. That she's a journalist doesn't change that fact. "Let's start over again. Who are you?"

She waits long enough that I can imagine the responses running through her mind. She wants to refuse to answer again. Ellie always did like a bit of verbal sparring, the push pull.

She was a journalist the whole time.

While I fucked her. While she ducked in and out of confidential client meetings.

It doesn't matter what she liked, she's a liar—and, I have no doubt, a thief. "Fine, if you don't want to answer me, let's loop back to five years ago—"

"My name is Melinda Gray," she snaps. "Are you happy?"

My mouth drops open. Ellie is *Melinda Fucking Gray?*

She smiles sweetly. "So you know who I am."

"Everyone in this city knows who you are," I growl. "You're the reason Gerome Lively went to jail."

She rolls her eyes. "No, but I helped."

Melinda Gray.

Nothing ever shocks me, but this... Wilson had tried to figure out who she was, too. Cole had no idea, either, and his sister-in-law was one of the sources for her book—not that they are close. Taylor has worked hard to rebuild her relationship with Hailey, but there's a lot of complicated history in the mix. And secrets, apparently.

But despite my grudging respect for Ms. Gray the writer, I can't forget that Ellie—Melinda—used me.

And she doesn't even try to deny it.

"So there you go. Now you know who I am," she says, her eyes glittering with challenge.

I shrug. "Sure. You're a pretty little liar."

She smirks. "Oh, Jason. You'll have to try harder than that to get my back up. I did what I had to do to get the story. And then you got lucky, and the story dissolved before I could write it."

"We turned into good guys, you mean."

"I wouldn't go that far."

"I would."

"Of course you would. You see yourself as the savior of the world. But we both know that's not true."

Oh, it's like that, is it? "And let me guess, you actually are? When you lie your way into the beds of—"

She cuts me off. "We never made it to a bed. But that wasn't a tactic."

That's true. I mostly fucked her on my desk. "Should I feel special?"

"If it makes you feel better."

"The way I see it, if it wasn't a tactic, that means we have unfinished business."

Her eyes go wide, and frankly, I know the feeling. What the fuck am I talking about?

As we've talked, I've closed the gap between us, and now I have her pressed against the wall again. I graze my thumb against her collarbone as I settle my hand on her shoulder. She tenses. "Relax," I murmur. "I'm not going to hurt you."

She laughs, a harsh little bark. "I'm not worried about that."

My thumb strokes back and forth. "I know. Why not?"

"History, maybe."

"Were you ever scared of me?"

"No." She follows that with a long, slow blink, and the pulse at the base of her neck flutters.

I lower my voice to a rough whisper. "I miss being inside you."

Her eyes open, blazing. "Fuck off."

"Any time, any place." I tug my tie loose. "Here sounds good."

"You don't trust me, but you want to—" She cuts herself off and slices the pink, wet tip of her tongue across her lower lip.

"Maybe I want to fuck you as a distraction, did you ever think of that?"

Her eyes narrow and the pink tongue disappears. "Probably one of the more honest things you've said to me."

"Nah. I told you," I say huskily. "I miss being inside you. I miss the sweet clutch of your pussy around my cock, I miss the breathy sounds you make when I suck on your tits, and I miss the way you pull my fucking hair when you come."

"I didn't." But the way her eyes widen again tells me she remembers it just as clearly as I do.

"Every single time. It's like you forget that you've got claws. And I love it."

"Rose-colored glasses," she murmured. "It wasn't that good. Besides, you've moved on to fancier flavors."

"I have?"

She bats her eyes and adopts a French accent. "We have such men in France as well, but we don't make movies about them."

That gasp I heard. I should have recognized it immediately. "That made an impression on you."

Ellie flips her hair. "It's fucking bullshit, that's all. The French absolutely make movies about their special operators."

I laugh, I can't help it. "You're pretending that you're mad her line was *inaccurate*?"

"Of course."

"And not that she was flirting with me."

"Why would I care about that?"

I drop my hand to her hip and grab a handful of her skirt in my fist. Her lips part and her eyes dilate, her pupils going inky black. "Because after all this time, you were jealous."

"Never." The word slips over her lush lower lip as a breathy whisper. "I couldn't care less who you try to fuck in your misguided pursuits—"

"I didn't fuck either of them."

"No?"

"I raced after you."

She clicks her tongue against her teeth. "Ooh, I didn't see you going soft, Jason."

My fist tightens and her skirt bunches higher on her hip. When I flex my little finger in an effort to cool-the-fuck-down, I graze bare flesh. Her thigh. "Nothing soft about me, *Ellie*."

Her gaze flares at the name. A reminder we have an unhealthy amount of baggage to sort out. "You chased after a ghost instead of finishing your mission."

I bare my teeth in what is undoubtedly a ghoulish grin. "Already had the information I needed."

"And that is?"

"None of your business."

"Okay." She rolls her eyes. "Well, this has been fun." She firmly sets her palm on my chest and pushes. "For real, though, I'm leaving now."

"Didn't get what you were looking for?"

She gives me a dismissive up and down. "I got something better. Now I know who's running damage control for Jeff Mayfair."

I growl under my breath as she gives me her back, moving to the door. I want to grab her and haul her to the sofa across the room. Instead, I watch her set that perfect little hand on the doorknob and twist it.

As the door opens, I find my voice. "The next time we see each other, Ellie—I want to finish this conversation."

She looks back at me. "It's Melinda. Maybe try using my real name and we'll see."

[8]
MELINDA

THE NEXT AFTERNOON, I use press credentials to get into an event for the very first time.

I never set out to be this kind of journalist. I've always wanted to write long-form narratives that take months to research and craft. But time is now of the essence, and it turns out that my Melinda Gray pseudonym—and a quick email from my agent—is enough to get credentialed for the Canadian Embassy lunch I couldn't otherwise get a ticket to. This is the endgame I was angling at for weeks.

I wear a blonde wig that matches the ID I have for Melinda Gray and pop on a pair of glasses, too. Not that the catering staff would notice or care if they saw me in the crowd, but one can never be too careful when one is juggling multiple identities.

Feeling very exposed, even in my disguise, I give my name to the security guard and hand over my bag to be searched. There's nothing out of line in there. A small laptop, a voice recorder, two cell phones, a wallet with Melinda Gray ID in it, a tube of dark plum lipstick, and a pack of gum.

The bag is handed around the metal detector I've just walked through, and I'm waved into the party.

My goal here is two-fold. I need to get close enough to the guest of honor, the Prime Minister's principal secretary, to send them a message by Bluetooth proximity. And if I can—

I skid to a stop as I round a corner.

In front of me is Jason Evans on the phone. He has his back to me, but I'd recognize the shape of him anywhere.

This is too much of a coincidence. I slow down, the chain of events replaying in my mind. Jason at the party, cozying up to the French Ambassador's wife. Did that have something to do with Mayfair, or is he playing another angle, for his own purposes.

Or another client.

Now that I know Jason is running interference for Mayfair, I know the story Kendra Browning asked about, the dump of information on wealthy people who Lively interacted with, has legs. What I can't figure out is what it might have to do with France and Canada.

Something stinks.

As I close the distance between us, I catch part of his conversation. Whoever he's talking to, he's reassuring them, his voice silky smooth. "Don't worry about it. The press is always sniffing in the wrong corners."

Well, if that isn't just the best cue for me to slide into view.

His gaze goes cold when he catches sight of me, and he ends the phone call.

I give him a light smile. "Is that what you think of us? Is it a general thought, or did you have any specific reporting in mind?"

He grabs me by the wrist and tugs me around his body, as if he's shielding me from the room I've just been standing in on my own two feet, like a grown-up. "You shouldn't be here."

The urge to roll my eyes is strong. "Why not?"

He doesn't have an answer for that. His jaw flexes in visible frustration.

"I'm a big girl, Jason."

His eyes glint, his gaze going steely as he moves closer. "Jason? You use my name like we're friends?"

We're definitely not. "I would never make that mistake."

His mouth twists. "Once upon a time, you called me Mr. Evans and listened to what I said."

We weren't friends then, either. "That was a role I was playing."

"For a story?"

"For reasons."

He's voice takes on an edge. "Was all of it a role? Play acting?"

Same line of questioning as yesterday. Fine. If he wants to ask that kind of question, I'll give him an answer. "Yes."

He sneers. "Liar."

What's new? "You think whatever you want. I'm working. Sniffing in the right corners, I promise you."

He watches me as I dart away. I feel his gaze on my skin, and it hurts. I miss the west coast. Being here in D.C. makes me feel empty inside, a hollow, angry shell that's dangerously brittle.

Secrets are security, but they're also walls that keep people out, and nothing makes that more obvious than having to run smack into one's past over and over again.

[9]

JASON

Jesus Christ, she shouldn't be here. I watch her disappear into the crowd. I don't need to chase after her right away—I saw her press badge, I know she's here legitimately.

But it's not safe.

Melinda Gray is anonymous for a reason. She's *persona non grata* in a lot of corners because of her investigations. I was up half the night devouring her words, searching for some understanding of what she might be working on now.

I came up blank, except for the obvious. She has a bullseye on my client. But everything we have found has underlined Mayfair's story. The photos are fake, and the blackmailer has now gone silent. In the five years since Melinda broke her first story—shortly after she left the Horus Group—she hasn't had a miss.

And Mayfair has nothing to do with this luncheon, so the fact she's here must be about another story, one I can't guess at. And yet it's important enough for her to show her face, albeit behind a blonde wig and a pair of glasses that stir me in the most inappropriate ways.

I've already had the meeting I was here for, a sit-down with the Prime Minister's principal secretary, who went to Harvard with my brother. When Mack sets me up on blind dates with people who have the ear of world leaders, I take the meeting—but this one was more small talk than anything.

I got the distinct impression that he didn't like me, in fact.

So I don't need to stay for lunch. I wasn't planning on it until I saw her. Now I make my way to a table just so I can keep my eye on the receptionist-turned-journalist who has gotten under my skin.

She isn't eating. Instead, she's set up a laptop at the side of the room and has buried herself in work. It looks like she's ignoring the room, although I don't assume that to be true for a second.

It still gives me a chance to observe her for a good while, and I like what I see. She's wearing a suit today, black pants and a jacket. Underneath it was a shock of red silk that looked loose and touchable when she appeared in front of me earlier. Now I can't see it, the way she's sitting, but I can see the curve of her thigh, and that gives me flashbacks that make it uncomfortable to sit with my legs too close together.

She was always fit and curvy, but in the last five years, she's gained a tough edge to her body that makes me want to spar with her. See what she might do if I pinned her to a mat and tried to force some answers out of her soft little mouth.

Not once during lunch do the people at my table try to make conversation with me, and that's just fine. As soon as my untouched plate is cleared, I make my way across to the studious journalist who lied her way onto my desk once upon a time.

She glances up when I stop beside her. Her gaze takes its time reaching my face. "Yes?"

"You really shouldn't be here."

"You already said that."

"You aren't going to ask me why?"

She puts her laptop away and stands. "No. Maybe you shouldn't be here, either, did you think of that?"

"I'm working."

"And so am I. We can do this all afternoon."

I try another tack, lightening my voice. "We need to stop meeting like this. Can we try again?"

She doesn't bite. "No. You need to stop telling me where I can and can't go, when I'm a grown-up and you're not the boss of me."

"I'm very aware I'm not the boss of you," I mutter. "That's not what I meant. If anything, I could protect you if you weren't so stubborn."

"That would almost certainly be a conflict of interest." She pulls out her phone, glancing at the screen before putting it away. "I'm leaving soon, if that makes you happy. I have a car coming to pick me up at the top of the hour."

I have watched her the whole time. She hasn't spoken to a soul. "What were you here for?"

"I had hoped to meet up with a source, but it couldn't happen because this guy who keeps following me got in the way." She says it in a deliberately bored voice that is obviously meant to get my back up.

It works. "I'm not following you. You keep showing up where I am. Maybe I should ask myself if *you* are following *me*?"

"And how would I know your schedule? You're the one with a professional hacker on staff."

"You think I had Wilson—" I'm officially mad now. "Listen, Ellie."

"Uh uh," she says softly. "We talked about this. My name is Melinda."

"Is it, though?" I match her soft tone. "Let's stop doing this in public, *Melinda*. Clearly, we have some issues to work through. Let's do it in private."

She gives me an appraising look before her eyelashes dust her cheeks. "Dinner?"

Too public still. "My place."

She laughs. "Okay, Captain Obvious. I'm not fucking you, so put that nonsense away."

"That's not what this is about. But I do want to protect you, and one day soon, you might need to trust me enough to let that happen."

"Because you want to fuck me."

"In spite of the fact that I want to fuck you. That's a complication, not a perk."

"Oh, it would be a perk."

"God fucking damn it, do you need to argue everything I say?"

"Yes," she says breathlessly, and that's when I catch it. The dilated pupils, the swollen lips. The drift toward me as we verbally spar. She wants this to be physical just as much as I do.

"What would it take?" I ask coarsely. "To get you alone in a room. Any room, your choice."

"An interview. On the record."

"With me?"

"With someone who knows the ins and outs of PRISM."

Literally any other answer would have shocked me less. I blink at her, sparring potential dropping quickly down the priority list. "That's your story? Mayfair has nothing to do with PRISM."

"That's something else. Will you comment on the record about Mayfair?"

"No."

"PRISM?"

"No."

"Jason—"

"Don't Jason me. You disappeared for five years, and now you think you can bat your eyelashes and get a quote from me? One that could kill my reputation in this town?"

"If my story is correct, this is bigger than protecting one's reputation." She shrugs. "And you were the one batting your eyelashes at me a minute ago. If you want to get me alone in a room, it'll be in a professional capacity."

And that's not happening.

Frustrated, I watch as she sweeps out of the room, a curious chameleon who manages to not capture anyone's attention. I don't get it. She's all I can see, but her little disguise complete with press pass works perfectly on everyone else.

I wait a beat, then follow her at a safe distance. By the time I get outside, she has disappeared from sight, which doesn't surprise me. But I don't see a hired car, either, and I wait, scanning the street for some sign of trouble.

Just before I turn to go back inside, a motorbike peels out. The helmet obscures the blonde wig, but the black suit is the same, and the shape of Ellie is unmistakable.

She's a beautiful liar, I think to myself as I watch her turn at the end of the street. Then I grind my teeth together, because those secrets could get her killed, and I can't let that happen.

[10]
MELINDA

THERE'S a certain stillness just before sleep that could be addictive. I don't sleep as much as other people, but there's a moment right before I drift off where I think, *I should do this more often*. Which is ridiculous because I do it every night, but only when I'm exhausted. When I fall into bed, my body aching with fatigue.

I'm drifting in that sweet spot, thinking of all the witty comebacks I could shove at Jason the next time we see each other, when my phone rings.

Rolling over, I grab it and peer at the screen. Caroline's name jumps off it.

"Hey," I say after hitting answer. "It's late."

"Help," she whispers.

I'm already on my feet. "Where are you?"

"Home. No cops."

Fuck. My heart slams against my chest. "I'm coming. I'm close, okay?"

"Okay." She groans.

One of the reasons I rented this apartment is that it's a block away from Caroline's place. I race down the stairwell, bursting onto the street level at top speed. I keep her on the line, knowing that I don't have another option. If a federal prosecutor says no cops, she means it for a terrible, no-good reason.

I have a key to her building, so I let myself in the side residents-only entrance and race up the stairs, listening the whole way for footsteps or any other sign that I'm not alone. I don't encounter anyone, and the fifth floor hallway is quiet, too.

But her door is ajar, which makes me want to throw up. Nudging it open, I carefully creep inside. I clear each room quickly, then find her in the bathroom, lying on the tiled floor, her blonde hair matted with blood and her clothes torn.

She moans when I say her name. "I'm sorry."

"What the fuck? You don't have anything to be sorry for." I crouch next to her and touch her wrist, quickly checking her pulse. "Can you stand?"

"My head hurts."

"Who did this to you?"

"I didn't see him."

"Why did you say no cops?"

"Maybe an...inside job..." Her eyelids drift shut.

"Oh no, Caro. We're not sleeping right now." I tap her cheek. "Wake up. Or I'm going to take you to the hospital."

"It hurts."

"That's what hospitals are for." I smile at her when she looks up at me. "Can I call your father?"

She flinches and shakes her head no.

"All right. You're going to be okay."

"I'm scared."

My best friend isn't scared of anything. Neither am I. That's what we bonded over. We're Valkyrie, we used to joke. But right now? I'm scared, too. "I have an idea. It's not a great idea, but..."

She gives me a faint smile. "I trust you."

Fuck, I hope this is the right thing to do.

The silence in the taxi is sharp and uncomfortable, because it's entirely possible this course of action is just as risky as the alternative.

I gaze out the wet, rain-dropped window, watching downtown Washington wake up oblivious to my best friend's pain.

This city is rocked by scandal on a weekly basis.

As a reporter, I cover the good, the bad, and the ugly.

The ugly is so much more common than anyone realizes. At any given moment, someone is drifting shell-shocked through everyone else's regular life, but at *this* moment, it's *my* someone, and that's so much harder than the academic understanding that bad things happen all the time.

Stiff and silent, Caroline sits beside me holding her jacket together. I tried to get her to change, but she'd been the smart one. "They'll need to take my clothes as evidence," she said.

So strong. I'd have crawled into the shower and washed it all away. Once upon a time, I'd have known better, but the last few years have done a number on me. On my faith in the system to treat any survivor with dignity, or to deliver any kind of justice when it comes to sexual assault.

We'd talked for a hot minute about going straight to the hospital or calling the metro police, but as much as we trust Detective Browning, it would only take one person slipping and the story would spin out of control.

So now we're going to the lions' den because they'll rip the heart out of anyone who dares to hurt us.

Two wrongs don't make a right. The saying felt like the truth until my friend was wronged.

Now I want vengeance.

Familiar nausea rises, threatening to paint the inside of the cab. My skin crawls at the thought of owing Jason a favor. But he'll find a way for Caroline to report this rape to the authorities on the quiet and get her in and out of a hospital without any media attention. He has all the connections I don't, that I could have had but gave up to be a rogue freelance journalist. Now I'm a nobody.

So despite all my misgivings, I gave the cabbie the address I know by heart.

Once upon a time, for a brief, hot summer, that address

held my hopes and dreams. Now... well, it's been a while since I've stepped through the door. So that complicates this a bit.

Never before has the phrase "the devil you know" been more appropriate.

I sigh and squeeze Caroline's hand, careful to avoid pressing on the nasty bruise developing around her wrist. She has a matching one around her neck, and while I haven't seen them, I know she's got matching ones on the insides of her thighs.

She should be able to call in the FBI to protect her here. She can't, and that makes my blood boil.

Vengeance looks pretty good right now.

I drive that thought deep, hiding it beneath what Caroline actually needs. Support and steadiness.

We turn the corner.

Cole Parker is in front of the building, watching for us. My former boss. He steps forward as the cab rolls to a stop and opens the door, helping Caroline out of the car. I can see his eyes taking in her battered appearance. The bruises. The ripped shirt. The scratches on her legs. She was wearing almost everything she'd had, except her underwear. *Because they'd been so badly torn, they'd fallen off her as she vomited into the toilet.* She'd told me to find her the big granny panties she wore when she was on her period, because she knew she'd be turning those over, too. I have the ripped ones in a Ziploc bag in the sling bag I wear across my body.

"Let's get you upstairs," he says quietly. A total contrast

to his bulky special forces build and the cold, killer stare he's perfected. I relax for the first time in two hours.

Their offices occupy the second and third floors of the three-story building, above a closed coffee shop, a 24-hour copy place, and a laundromat. Nothing has changed in five years.

Well, everything has changed.

But their offices are the same.

We take the waiting elevator, the seconds ticking by quietly as we ascend to the third floor. Cole uses his keycard to open the doors when we arrive.

As soon as the elevator doors open, I know Jason is here. I can't look at him just yet, so I fix my gaze on the familiar space. Behind the desk—*my* desk, once upon a time, before I fucked everything up by taking my panties off for the man I'm not looking at, and fell for him, and gave up the first scoop of my career—is a passive-looking young fellow.

Is he who he says he is? Would they ever be tricked again? No. Jason would have been furious when he discovered I wasn't the community-college-grad Ellie. Livid that he hadn't seen through my documents, that the fake ID I'd paid so handsomely for had actually put one over on the great Horus Group brain trust.

Pivoting, I sweep the lobby until I register where Jason is standing in the doorway to the main conference room. What is he thinking? Did he ever miss me here, or was I nothing once I was gone—collateral damage. Cut losses.

Two can play that game. I keep going, seeing what's the

same and what's different in the space, but I stop my assessment before I get to his office at the end of the hall where we first had sex.

His hands on my hips, inching my skirt up to my waist. The wet press of his mouth on my neck. The hard brand of his—

"Ellie," he says, his voice hard and sharp.

This was a mistake.

I swallow hard and finally look at him, at the two black coals staring back at me, and at the hard flex of his jaw.

"Would you be more comfortable in the conference room or my office?" Jason manages to keep his burning gaze on me and still seem genuinely concerned for Caroline at the same time. He's got mad manipulation skills, I give him that.

"I don't care." Those are the first words she's uttered since I told her who I was calling. Caro's never met Jason before. She didn't know that I worked here until I quit, until I confessed I'd fallen for someone I'd meant to investigate, and I needed to get out of town.

She doesn't know all of what this is costing me, but she knows enough, and even in distress, she's got my back.

Jason points to the conference room, and I take Caro's arm. He waits for us to pass, then follows behind. I can feel the heat of his hand at the small of my back—not touching, but close.

Cole leads the conversation, for which I'm supremely grateful. Jason sits at the far end of the table, slightly out of

Caroline's field of vision, and he takes notes as Cole calmly leads her through what they need to know and what could wait for the doctors.

"How much of a circus is this going to be?" Caroline's voice shakes.

I see Cole and Jason exchange a look. They're thinking, *good, she knows the risk, she's smart to ask.*

Cole doesn't miss a beat, he just waits for us to give him our attention again and he nods. "It's going to be a circus. Big time. But on your terms. And we'll be standing behind you, or beside you, or in front of you. Wherever you want us to be, whatever you need us to do."

All of that standing sounds expensive. And the Horus Group doesn't work for people like Caroline Denten pro bono.

I lean forward. "How much will that cost? She doesn't want her family making any decisions. If you help us beyond this meeting, Caroline's the client."

"Of course." Cole doesn't look down the table, but he waits a beat to see if Jason wants to weigh in. When he doesn't, that must have meant something, because Cole leans back. "We'll need a ten-thousand-dollar retainer."

I do a double-take. I'm not sure what I'm surprised about more—that they want money, or that it's so little.

I mean, it's *not*. It's a ridiculous amount of money to pay ex-soldiers to hold your hand while you go to the hospital and the police station and run the gauntlet of media once they catch wind of the story.

. . .

***Federal Prosecutor Victim of a Home Invasion;
the Granddaughter of a former Speaker of the
House accuses her own team of not protecting
her while she's pursuing a sealed indictment
against a protected Individual***

It's a story that demands a circus.

"I can get a bank draft in a few hours," I say, and Caroline protests, but I just rub her shoulder and repeat myself. "Really, it's fine."

Cole clears his throat. "We'll return whatever funds we don't use at the end of this."

There won't be any funds left. They will exhaust the retainer by the end of the week, which is why it is usually ten times that amount. *Was* usually, I suppose. I don't know what they're charging these days, but they don't look like they're running a charity.

"The next step..." Cole continues, detailing how they'd send someone ahead to the hospital and arrange for Caroline to bypass the Emergency Department, going straight to the Sexual Assault and Domestic Violence Assessment Unit. She'll see a social worker, a nurse, and a doctor if she had any significant injuries, and a rape kit will be collected. "At that point, it's up to you if you want to involve the police immediately."

"I don't." Caro sits up a little straighter, the prosecutor trying to take back some control over what happened to the woman.

"Then as you know, the rape kit is stored securely, transferred through to the police lab with an anonymous identification number. The evidence is collected, but your name isn't attached to it yet." He glances at his watch. "Have you slept at all?"

"No." Her voice is barely above a whisper now, but she keeps going and it breaks my heart.

"Ms. Denten, you aren't our first client who's been through this," Jason says from the end of the table, and his voice is like ice. Barely controlled fury simmers under the surface, I realize with a shock, and I don't know how I didn't pick up on it before. *That's why he sat so far away.*

God, this must be so inconvenient for him. My own rage quickly rises, and I pinch back a sneer. "Good to know," I say instead, my voice suddenly frigid as well.

Cole frowns at me, then at his partner, and finally offers Caroline an almost-smile. "We need to give Wilson thirty minutes to get ahead of us to the hospital. Would you like something to eat?"

She shakes her head. "Could I lie down?"

"Of course. We'll give you both the room, and come back when it's time to go." Cole stands and walks the long way around the table, collecting Jason at the far end of the table and ushering the still-glowering ice man out of the room.

What is he afraid we'll do to his conference room? I wrap a protective arm around my friend and guide her to the couch. She sags against me, and we hug for a minute, holding on to each other tighter than we have in...as long as I can remember.

I hear heavy footsteps and glance back over my shoulder. Jason has returned, but he hasn't come back to do battle. He's holding a blanket, which I gratefully take. Caroline lies down and curls up in it, closing her eyes, and I stand there for a minute, just looking at her.

"We'll need to take this with us to the hospital," she mumbles.

Jason clears his throat. "Yep, we know."

Then he catches my eye.

I raise one eyebrow. "Yes?"

He tips his head toward the hall. Right, outside would be better. I lead the way, and when I stop just outside the door, his hand lands in the small of my back. No ghosting of a touch this time, it's solid contact—warm, startling, and familiar in the same way his scent was. He propels me forward and I twist away from him, a protest rising to my lips. "Caroline..."

"She's safe. Maybe she needs a minute to herself more than she needs you hovering." He drags the words out like I'm a five-year-old, and it pisses me off. I don't need much. I'm a bundle of dry kindling, rough on all sides, begging for a match.

"You have no idea what she needs," I spit out as we reach his office at the end of the hall.

"Yes, I do. That's why you're here. That's why you didn't go to anyone else, or try to do this yourself. Because you know that I *do* get it, that I *can* guide her through what is going to be an agonizing journey, and you hate that as much as you're thankful for it, too."

He clicks the door shut behind us and I freeze at the sudden intimacy of being alone together. That ridiculous thought doesn't last long, though.

From behind me, he takes a deep breath, and I can hear the freight train of conflict approaching. "I need to search you."

"Excuse me?"

"You've all but admitted one of my clients is the subject of a story you're working on."

"Not if he's not guilty."

"Guilty of what?"

I shake my finger at him. "Nope. We're not doing this. I escorted Caroline here because she needs you. I don't need you. Feel free to walk me out."

He doesn't move. "Why us? Knowing that I would be suspicious of your motives to get inside these offices."

I unclench my jaw. "Because you're the best." It's not a lie. But the truth is that I didn't know where else to go. Despite our clashes, when I saw Caroline on the bathroom floor, I was deeply grateful that calling Cole was an option.

Jason watches me, his expression unreadable, then he nods. "This is what we do. We'll keep her safe. Is there anything else I need to know? Why aren't her parents here, for real?"

Tension crawls up my back, stealing any diplomatic

answer I might have been able to offer. This time, it's the unvarnished truth that Jason gets, whether he believes it or not. "Because they would kill this story and make her keep it a secret forever."

I don't think it's possible for his lips to pull any tighter, to get any more pinched, but they do. The curve of his top lip turns white as he fights to hold back whatever he wants to say next. Fuck him.

"By cutting them out of this, you're inviting more drama. Unnecessary drama."

"Thanks for the lesson in family dynamics, but it wasn't my call, it was hers."

"You said you didn't want them to kill your story."

"That's not what I said. I would never write about Caroline's assault. I'm not a journalist here."

"This is your beat."

"*Her* story is not my beat."

"Sexual assault at the highest levels."

I want to throw something at his head. My fists, maybe, or reality. "You have no idea why I write the stories I write."

His eyes glittered as he thought about what he was going to say next. I should have seen it coming, really. He leads with a quote I recognize. "*For a six-figure retainer fee —and probably a hefty slice of your soul, as well—The Horus Group will be on anyone's side.* I think I have a good idea about why you wrote *that*."

I smirk. "So you've read my work."

"Just tonight. After you left the party. I thought I should do some oppo-research for my client."

I ignore that jab. Right now, I'm not working and I can't think about the fact that Jeff Mayfair is one of his clients. But we need to get something straight. "Think whatever you want about me. But until two hours ago, Caroline thought she was safe and protected by her team. That's why I came to you, that's why I'm standing here. So if you need to know anything about me to clear the air between us, just ask. I'm an open book."

If I thought he was icy before, that was nothing. The air crystallizes around us, sharp and frigid. Ice like knives. "You are not an open book," he whispers. "Don't lie to me again and we'll be fine. As you say, Caroline deserves justice. We'll get that for her, one way or another."

"Not the other." I swallow hard. That's another lie and we both know it. "I'm not asking you to do your thing."

His eyes narrow. "What do you think you know about *my thing?*"

My heat thumps hard in my chest. "I worked here, remember?"

"You were the receptionist. And you were investigating us the entire time. Do you think I'm going to dignify your suggestion that anything we do here is unethical or illegal with *any* kind of response?"

Almost everything they do has a tinge of illegality to it. Who's the liar now? "We're permanently off the record, Jason. Don't feed me a line like that."

He stalks toward me and I stand my ground until he stops close enough for me to breathe in his scent. "Do you trust me to protect Caroline?"

I nod. I don't trust him in any other regard, but I know to the depth of my soul that he'll keep my friend as safe as possible.

"Then maybe it would be best for both of us if you let me do that. I'll work better if you aren't here."

His words feel like an actual slap to my face. "No. I don't care if you don't like me, or if you think I'm causing trouble—"

"That's not what this is about."

"Then you'll—"

He cuts me off by sliding his hand into my hair, his fingertips dragging little zaps of lightning across the skin on my neck. "You distract me."

"What does that—"

This time I'm cut off by a knock at the door, and it echoes through the room like a double tap of gun shots. Jason's hand tightens on the nape of my neck. "Yeah?"

"Wilson's good to go," Cole says from the other side of the closed door, but we can hear him clearly. Which means he might have heard us, and that makes my face turn red. I'm not even sure what it is we're talking about, but I'm pretty sure it has to do with the terribly inconvenient chemistry zinging between us.

"We're just having a battle of wills over the matter of Caroline's account, we'll be right there." Jason glowers at me. Okay, so we're agreed on the inconvenient part. He drops his voice. "We don't have a lot of time, so I'll just lay it out for you. When Cole told me you called because of a rape, I lost my fucking mind. And now I feel like an asshole for being grateful it wasn't you. Caroline doesn't deserve that. I'm going to destroy whoever hurt her. I'll do it for free. And I can't have you judging me with your pretty dark gray eyes while I'm doing it."

[11]

MELINDA

Jason's confession is still echoing in my mind hours later, when we leave the hospital through the service entrance.

True to their word, they've kept Caroline safe the whole time. Now we're going back to their offices to regroup and decide on the next step. Cole wants to find a safe house of their own and hire a private team to protect her.

Jason doesn't agree.

"I think we should call in the U.S. Marshals. We can go outside your division, outside the normal reporting chains if need be. But the longer we leave them out of the loop, the more questions they are going to have about why," he says to Caroline. Grudgingly, I have to admit I like the way they include her in the conversation. They recognize that she has a unique perspective here as both a victim and a professional in this area herself.

She plays with the sleeve of her sweatshirt. She got to shower and change at the hospital, and came out of the bathroom looking determined and fierce—every inch the prosecutor that she is. "Do you have a contact in mind?"

"Deacon Webb. He's former Secret Service. Recently left the president's detail. I would trust him with my life."

Caroline glances over at me. I don't know what to do. "You could stay with me," I say, but the uncertainty is clear in my voice. "It's not ideal, though."

I want her surrounded by real life GI Joes. I'm clever and fast, but a bodyguard I am not.

She squares her shoulders. "I'll talk to him. Let's start with that. We can document the case at the very least, and making a random connection outside the division is low risk."

Her logic makes sense. There would be no way it would make any sense for this Deacon person to be lying in wait for Caroline. And marshals have a better network of resources than the Horus Group does, at least on their own.

Jason has access to significant resources through his half-brother, but that relationship is complicated. "I agree," I tell her quietly. "For what that's worth."

She squeezes my hand. "It's worth everything."

———

Two hours later, the cavalry arrives. Deacon Webb has a terrifying presence, a sharp machine of a man, and yet there's something about him that is soothing and calming, too.

It turns out he and Caroline have a mutual acquaintance in common, a prosecutor in the financial crimes division out in California, and through that short handed code they immediately bond.

"We'll keep her safe," he promises me, and I believe him. "Nobody outside of my team will know we have her."

Wilson works up a digital cover story that has Caroline in the hospital with appendicitis, then she makes a couple of carefully worded phone calls to people on her team. Exhaling after the last one, she puts her phone down on the table. "And if anyone was tracking those, they look like they came from the hospital?"

Wilson nods, then pockets the phone. "I'll keep it charged and pinging off that repeater until we've found who did this to you."

"Magic," she says weakly. "Before we go, can I have a minute alone with Melinda?"

They nod and excuse themselves. She glances around the room. It's almost certainly wired. I pull out my phone and play some dance music at top volume. She leans in, her lips right next to my ear. "If I don't make it out of this alive, there's a safe deposit box with your name on it."

Fear wraps its fist around my throat. We don't have time to dig into the why of that. We should have compared notes weeks ago, but she swore an oath to work within the law.

Taking a deep breath, I squeeze her tight. "That won't be necessary. Now go and be safe."

A shudder racks through her body, and she gets up. She doesn't walk all the way to the door, though. She stops, her eyes wide. "We'll get coffee soon, right?"

"A full night of drinks, I promise."

She gives me a bittersweet smile. "Do you ever think, if maybe we had made a different decision back then..."

Every single day. "You're going to be okay, Caro. I'm going to get him."

———

I'm still waiting in the boardroom when Jason returns —alone.

"She's off?"

He nods.

I turn back to the bank of dark screens on the wall. "You've had a tech upgrade in the last five years."

"Some things have changed, yeah."

I ran my fingers under the table, looking for the button to turn the screens on. "And some things have stayed the same." I frown at the dossier there. It's my own. "Not funny, Jason."

"We're nothing if not thorough." He walks past the screens and waves at my headshot. "Although we don't have many details on our newest client's closest friend..."

"What other dossiers have you pulled for her case?"

"That's classified." He sits next to me. Close enough for

me to see that he's got a full day of stubble on his jaw now. Close enough that when he turns his gaze on me, I feel the full weight of his piercing blue eyes. "What do you know that you might want to add to the investigation?"

"Nothing." My reply is instantaneous and truthful. I *know* very little. I have my instincts, and loose pieces that almost fit together, but nothing is sure right now.

"You know what I'm going to say. We can't help clients who keep things from us."

"I'm not your client," I say softly.

"You're her best friend."

"And an investigator in my own right."

Jason frowns. "That's what concerns me."

I change the subject. "Do you ever worry about having a conflict of interest between clients?"

"Yes." A muscle twitches in his jaw. "Do I have a conflict of interest that you think I should know about?"

"That's not my job."

"What *is* your job, exactly?"

"We've been over this."

"Did you go to journalism school?"

"What does Wilson say?"

"He tells me I should stop obsessively thinking about you."

"Smart man."

He gets up and paces. After a few silent minutes, he gestures toward the kitchenette. "I'd offer you something to eat, but it may not be up to your standards."

I blink at him. "I don't have standards."

He frowns. "The bagels and muffins?" He groans. "Of course that was an act."

"No, that was a job. And an act, sure, if we're being literal. But aren't all jobs acts on some level? I haven't slept properly in a very long time. Most days, I run on coffee, salad, and sandwiches, all prepared by other people. Whatever you have is fine. A granola bar sounds grand."

His hand clenches into a fist on the table. "How long has it been since you had a good meal?"

The night before I left Malibu. "A while."

"Can I buy you breakfast?"

I should say no. I want to say no, but I want to say yes even more. And right now, I'm too tired to deprive myself of a good meal, even if it comes with complicated company. "Sure. Why the fuck not?"

He gives me a faint smile. "That's the spirit."

It's early enough that when we arrive at a diner a block away, we have a booth to ourselves with a healthy amount of distance from any other customers.

The coffee is good and our food comes quickly, and Jason lets me refuel in quiet. It's not until I slow down and put my fork down, my plate mostly clear, that he starts a conversation. "Yesterday, you asked me about PRISM."

I'm genuinely surprised that he's voluntarily returning to that subject. "Is this breakfast on the record?"

He doesn't look amused. "Nothing is ever on the record between us. Got it?"

I roll my eyes. "Got it."

"What do you know about it? Why were you asking?"

"I know enough, and it's deep research for a story. You seemed surprised when I brought it up."

"It's not like they have Wikipedia page."

"I spent years investigating Gerome Lively and Amelia Dashford Reid."

"Is that what brought you here in the first place?"

"Here?" I glance around the diner.

"D.C."

"The first time or the second time?"

"Now."

I hesitate. "Yes."

His eyebrows hit the roof. "Is that a little bit of truth that I hear, Ellie?"

I shrug. "If we're trading information, it's only fair."

"I'm not the enemy here."

"That remains to be seen." I play with a sugar packet. "I know about the incriminating documents."

His expression doesn't change. "What documents?"

"If you don't know, I'm not going to tell you any more than that."

That gets me a small twitch on his temple. "You're fishing."

"I'm not. I know that there are many people implicated, and I also know there are bad actors floating false flag reports, too."

That gets a bigger reaction. His jaw rocks to the side, then he leans in. "I'm very interested in that part of it."

"Mayfair?"

"No comment."

"Jason—"

"I can't. If I could, I would. But let me make some calls later, while you sleep, and I'll see if I can share more later today." He gives me a charming grin. "Over dinner?"

"Two meals in one day is really asking a lot."

"I'll ask again after you get some rest."

"I'm fine."

"No heroics. So we're going to keep going about our business like last night didn't happen, but you cannot pursue any investigation without checking in with me first." Jason catches my chin in his hand. "Can you do that?"

How am I supposed to know what will come up? "Sure. Yes."

He doesn't look like he quite believes me—smart man—but he accepts my answer. "Good. Who knows where you live?"

"Nobody."

"You haven't taken anyone home, even a total stranger?" When I raise my eyebrow at the question, he doesn't back down. "I don't care. I'm asking as a security specialist."

"*Nobody*. Not even Caroline, although she knows I'm in her neighborhood. I—I got some death threats when I released my book. I was anonymous before that, but once those came in, to my publisher and my agent, we took extra steps. My home in California, this apartment...they're rented by numbered corporations, which can't be traced back to me."

"That's slick."

"I take my privacy very seriously." Even as I look at the bottom of my second cup of coffee, I realize I'm bone tired. And suddenly, I'm done with Jason not believing me. "Come on. You want to be the first person to know where I live?"

He throws some bills on the table to cover our breakfast. "After you."

We loop back to his office to get his car and I give him the address.

He nods approvingly. "Good location."

He repeats the sentiment once we park and I lead him in the side entrance and up to my apartment, which probably doesn't look anything like what he thought his Ellie's space might look like. I'm not her, though. I'm the girl with Spartan taste and few belongings. The bed is still rumpled from when I jumped out of it last night, but I don't care. I'm more interested in showing him the view out my windows.

"See?" I grin. "Who would try to break in through the back, and get caught on camera by the US Navy?"

He moves in behind me to follow my pointing finger. "Smart."

"I try."

"You succeed." He says it grudgingly, but there's enough warmth in his words that I believe him.

He moves his attention from the view to the desk space in front of the window, and Monica. "And you have a plant. That's properly domestic."

I don't tell him that I named the aloe vera. "It's good for cuts and bruises."

His gaze narrows. "Do you get a lot of those?"

"I joined a CrossFit gym."

"Liar," he mutters.

I shrug. "I have a brand and I like to be consistent."

"Dishonesty?"

"With you? It has its benefits." I have to keep him on his toes.

He swears under his breath. "I need to go back to the office. Can you promise me you'll stay here and get some sleep?"

I'm going to fall into that bed the second he leaves. Not that he's made any move toward the door. He's still standing right next to me. "I'm working a story."

"You promised—"

"Not Caroline's story," I burst out, pivoting so we're facing each other. "Jesus Christ, Jason. I told you—"

"How am I supposed to trust—"

I cut him off with a furious kiss. I jam my mouth against his and my heart leaps into my throat. His lips part in surprise, a sweet, soft brush of still-familiar flesh, and I pull back. He glares at me, and that makes two of us that are struggling to process what I just did.

"I shouldn't have—"

He's the one to cut me off this time, his mouth hard and hungry against mine. His tongue seeks mine out, and our bodies have no trouble at all figuring out what comes next. My breasts swell, my nipples tightening, and I arch into his touch as he trails his fingers down my neck and across my fabric covered chest.

Yes, yes.

My hands reach for his hips, the tight muscles of his ass, and I pull him against my core. He's hard for me already, and I rub against his erection.

He groans, his mouth on my neck now. "We can't do this."

"Obviously." I wait a beat. "Your hand is on my tit, though."

He tightens his fingers around my eager nipple. "What's your fucking point?"

"It might seem that despite our agreed upon decision, we're doing it anyway." I shove him away, but he doesn't get very far, because his other hand is tangled up the back of my shirt, palming my side.

He squeezes my flesh hard enough to make me gasp. Memories flash through my mind. The same sound, the same squeeze. Different time, different place.

Jason never fucked me in anger before. He always let me take the lead, and it was me that seduced him with cunning and ease. Surprisingly sweet, not-so-surprisingly effective. I liked him back then. I don't like him anymore.

He's proven himself kind—but I knew that. The thing is, I'm older now. Jaded. Brittle to the bludgeon of truth that it doesn't matter how *kind* a man is if he's also a criminal. A henchman of the worst sort.

A murderer—or at best, an apologist for murderers.

The biggest mistake I ever made was falling for him. I won't do that again. But use him for some stress relief? I can do that. And it's even better if he's mean about it.

"I need a shower," I whisper as he hauls me back into his arms.

"You think I fucking care about that after five years?"

I cry his name. He swallows it, then my next sound as well.

He grips my hair in a gentle fist and tugs us apart. Then he gives me the sternest fucking look I've ever seen. "I want you bent over the bed. That's how I liked you best, remember?"

My thighs shake. I remember just fine. Never a bed, but he did like to bend me over his desk, plant one of his solid hands on my back to hold me down, and pound me from behind. I liked it, too.

"I want your ass in the air so high your pussy aches from being exposed to me."

I always did like his filthy mouth. Both for the words it can string together and the way it moves against my skin. The chemistry between us hasn't changed in my absence. If anything, it's even more incendiary now than when I was his dirty little office secret.

But he wasn't the only one keeping filthy lies to themselves.

He's still not.

This is a terrible idea. I don't care. He strips me naked and I crawl onto the bed, presenting myself to him shamelessly. I need this. I need an escape, I need to slither back into an old version of myself that could do this with wild abandon.

See me.

Want me.

Need me.

Take me.

Of course it's not that simple. Tomorrow we'll be at odds again, but right now, I'm a body in need of pleasure and Jason's brand of punishing fucks delivers precisely what I want.

He swats lazily at my ass, then my thighs, wordlessly correcting my pose. I get a pleased squeeze when my cunt is shoved up enough, then his fingers slide between my eager wet folds.

I'm already soaked for him, a needy mess, but he doesn't rush this part.

Fingering me was always Jason's preferred foreplay. Sometimes it was the whole deal. He would get me off, then carry the scent of me on him as he went about his business.

I think it's more than that, though. I think there's something about putting his fingers inside my body that is even more intimate for him than fucking me with his cock. Right now, he's behind me and I can't see him, but I can imagine that he's watching, hypnotized by the view of his fingers sliding in and out of my pink hole. Stretching me, taking up space where it literally didn't exist until he pushed those thick fingers into my pussy.

It's a head game for him. His fingers, a cunt he's going to ruin with his cock. I feel tight around his fingers, however will his massive dick fit... But even as I mock that a little in my head, I squirm against his slow, thrusting digits. The head game works on me, too.

I love being destroyed by him. I love the way he stretches me and consumes me.

"Jesus," he breathes.

And I realize the dirty talk had drifted away, that we were both just panting now. Needy, horny, and way too emo for my liking.

"Fuck me, Jason," I breathe. He liked it when I used his name. I'm never above manipulating him for my own purposes. "I want to feel it. Make me feel it."

He growls and rolls me over, roughly, then looms above me. He's naked now, a beast of a man. Rippling muscles and a heavy, rigid cock. He has a condom on, and that's all I can see—the club he's going to impale me with, and oh how I've missed this. *I've missed him.* The realization ripples through me like a bladed shiver. It's a dangerous thought. I can contain it, of course. I'm made of sterner stuff than melting desire. I can want Jason right now, savor all the horrible things he'll do to my body, and still walk away.

I have to be able to walk away.

Missing him is just the price of having had him inside me.

I close my eyes and rock my hips up into his hands. *Fuck me*, I say, but it's probably just inside my head. Maybe it would be better if we don't talk, if I just give him my body to do with what he will.

I feel him drag his cock through my wetness, up to my clit, then back again to my entrance. I whimper in anticipation, then he thrusts, and I make the same sound again because the anticipation was accurate.

He's so big, and it's so good.

He fills me to the point of too much, until I think my skin might break apart from the sensations, and then he stops.

"Look at me," he growls.

I roll my hips, urging him on. *Fuck me. Take me.*

He grips my face in his hand. "Look. At. Me."

"Fuck me." I say it out loud now, my eyes flashing open and grabbing his gaze. That's the deal, that's what we're doing here.

"I need you to stay safe," he growls. "And you can't come until you promise me that you'll do that."

"Fuck *you*," I spit. I can get myself off, I don't need him for anything. Not that, not security. Nothing. "This isn't why I kissed you. We make no deals."

He rolls his hips and buries himself deep to the root again. "Come on," he cajoles.

"Not like this," I whisper. "Please." Every emotion possible has spiraled through me in a hot second. Anger, sadness, fear, hunger. *Happiness.* "Don't make this about something I can't promise."

"Ellie," he groans.

"Just fuck me."

He swears under his breath and thrusts his hips, but he's holding back.

I want more. I want him to turn me into a pathetic,

drooling mess. I want him to wring me out, leave me broken and haunted with good memories instead of bad.

I want, I want.

I can't have.

This is it, this has to be enough. I need to let my guard down this once because I never can again. "This isn't fair," I mutter, and he laughs. Gently, and...lovingly, in a way. For Jason. I close my eyes, say a prayer, then look at him. "I'll be as safe as I possibly can."

He strokes my cheek as he moves again. "Who are you?"

"Just a girl asking a boy to get her off," I quip.

He kisses me. I shudder against him and go as soft as I can, welcoming his tongue, his hands, his cock. All of him, in all of me.

I'm Ellie, I want to tell him. Part of me is still Ellie. But it's so much more complicated than that, so I let it go and close my eyes again. I give in to the sensations of his body on top of mine, our first time in a bed.

Our last time, almost certainly. I don't want it to end, and it doesn't, not for a while. He fucks me like he knows it too, until the urge to come apart is too great and suddenly my orgasm is upon us. I clutch my limbs around him, grinding my clit against his pelvic bone as he thunders to follow me in climax.

When he falls beside me on the bed, I glance across him and out the window. We fucked through dawn, and now it's bright out.

He scrubs a hand over his face. "I should let you get some rest."

I could invite him to stay and sleep next to me, but I can't handle what that would unlock. "I'll triple chain the door after you leave."

It's the only acknowledgment of what he tried to make me promise during sex. He doesn't reply.

[12]
JASON

Our client is a quarter of the way around the world right now, having left D.C. immediately after his fundraiser. He makes himself available on video as soon as I message him, though, which I like.

Cole joins me for the call. The two of us are in our boardroom and Jeff Mayfair is in a room in his estate in England.

"Jeff, we've had an interesting development," I begin. "We've made contact with a journalist, Melinda Gray. You can look her up. She's the one who wrote that book about Gerome Lively that led to his arrest."

He makes a note on a pad of paper.

"Ms. Gray has requested an interview with me, which of course I declined. But over the last couple of days, our paths have crossed a few times, and I have good reason to believe she can be trusted—not on the record, I assure you. But for deep background purposes, I'd like your authorization to share some of what Wilson has discovered. Not the images you shared with us. Perhaps the emails—redacted— and the banking routing numbers. I think she may have information that could help our investigation, but I need to show her some of our hand first."

"And do you trust her?"

That's a big question. I ignore the images flashing through my mind. Her body twisting beneath mine, the fierce look in her eye as I gripped her jaw, the softness that immediately followed her stunning release. Do I trust Ellie? It depends. But the question is moot, as I don't think *she* trusts anyone, and that kind of fear is dangerous. "I think we can manage the sharing of information, with safeguards to protect you. And if we can gain any insights at all from her, it will be worth it. There are a lot of moving pieces here, and I think she has a different angle on the situation than we do."

"All right. Make it happen. Carefully."

Cole clears his throat. "Jeff, there's one other thing we want to discuss. And again, this falls under our confidentiality and non-disclosure agreement, although we understand you may not be able to comment. But we want you to know that it is on our radar that you are being talked about as a potential PRISM council member."

The billionaire on the other end of the line doesn't react.

My heart sinks.

Cole doesn't react, but the silence on our end of the line is palpable, too.

Mayfair frowns. "On your radar, how?"

Cole smiles politely—but coolly. "That's confidential for other reasons, sir."

"It's not true." Mayfair clips the three words out, sharp and short. It's the first time I've seen emotion seep into his demeanor. "I don't want to get Scott involved, but let's just say, there is no love lost in our family for that organization."

"There's a summit this weekend..." I trail off. Leading.

Jeff gestures at what looks like a very old, very expensive tapestry hanging on the wall behind him. "And I'm nowhere near Hilton Head, am I?"

"So you're aware of it."

"Aware of it for the singular purpose of avoiding it, yes. In the same way I went out of my way to not do business with Lively, too. There's overlap there, as I know you are aware."

"We are aware."

He pauses, then leans in to the camera. "We are in turbulent times, Mr. Evans and Mr. Browning. But there is no safety in being suspicious of absolutely everyone. We also need to choose who to trust. I'm choosing you, and Ms. Gray. Show her whatever you want, including the photos. This has gone beyond damage control if I'm being used as cover for whatever PRISM is up to."

[13]

MELINDA

I wake up mid-afternoon and drag myself into a shower. Between the sleepless night of worry about Caroline and the unexpected but brutally satisfying sex reunion with Jason, I feel like I've been run over by a truck. Steam, soap, and then sliding into a belted caftan for a coffee run all help me feel a bit more human.

But my bravado that maybe everything is going to be fine only lasts until I step outside, and I find Jason waiting for me, leaning against the side of his car.

"I don't need a babysitter," I tell him.

He raises an eyebrow, either at my premise or choice of words, I'm not sure. I don't care. Frustration swells in my chest.

I gesture at the car, and his suit, and the sweltering heat of the late D.C. summer shimmering around us. "How long have you been waiting here?"

"Half an hour." He points to the passenger door. "Get in."

"Why didn't you call me?" Except I know why.

"It turns out, I don't have your number."

"Weird."

He shrugs. "I was waiting for Wilson to track down one of your neighbors when you came downstairs."

"I was just going to get some food. We didn't make it into my kitchen, but the cupboards are quite bare."

"We can pick something up on the way. Or get delivery."

"And where do you think you're going to take me?"

"The office. Wilson has some things to show you."

I hesitate. "Something good?"

"I'm not wasting your time, Ellie. Get in the car."

———

We don't talk about our early morning boundary-obliterating sex. We don't talk at all as he navigates through the busy afternoon traffic, or on the quiet and quick elevator ride up from the parking garage to the third floor.

It's reassuring, actually. This isn't Jason vs. Ellie, this is Melinda Gray being invited to the Horus Group offices for a reason that isn't yet clear.

We don't go to the boardroom. Instead, Jason leads me to Wilson's cavelike command central of an office. He's the only partner who doesn't have a window, by his own preference.

Jason stops me at the door. "How do you feel about signing an NDA?"

I jut my chin at him. "I'd rather try my luck with the wi-fi at the coffee shop downstairs and whatever teenage hackers I can find on Reddit, thanks."

He sighs. "I thought that would be your answer. So I'm going to ignore you said that and tell you some shit anyway, because maybe the only way to get you to trust me is to show my trust in you. But everything you see and hear in this office is off the record, background only. Understand?"

I nod.

Inside, the hacker is waiting for us. Spread out over three screens are the contents of a classic Horus Group dossier.

Jeff Mayfair, their client.

And one of the screens shows Mayfair with a young girl, too young to be in a photo with a grown man. I recognize the setting immediately. "That's Lively's private plane."

"Hello to you, too," Wilson says. "And you're correct."

"You don't think the photo is real."

"Mayfair insists that it's not, and we believe him. He has provided comprehensive travel records, and there is zero overlap with Lively. In fact, Jeff had gone out of his way over the years to avoid Lively, which makes targeting him an interesting and not particularly well-thought-out decision."

"Interesting." I scour the other screens. "Was the blackmail all via email?"

"Yep. And it dropped off immediately when we had Mayfair get ahead of the NDA story."

"I thought that had your fingerprints on it. So he's not running for office?"

"Never." Wilson smirks.

"Who else has been blackmailed?"

They don't answer. I look back and forth between Jason and Wilson. "Do you not know of any other targets, or you can't say?"

"We don't have any other clearly identified targets. But we suspect there are others."

"Of course there are others." I think hard about how much I want to share. Protecting my story isn't just about getting the headline, or not wanting to be scooped. It's about who gets to control the narrative. And these two are kings at twisting narratives to suit their purposes. "There are rumors Lively had a massive document collection. Video, photographs, emails. But it didn't come out in discovery, and now that he's dead there's no reason for the Feds to keep it private—and from some of my sources, I'm told they have told survivors that they don't have it. They believe it's just a rumor."

Jason's jaw twitches. "Is that what Caroline was working on?"

"No."

He eyes my rapid response with suspicion. "Are you sure?"

"She didn't work on Lively's case. Wrong jurisdiction.

He didn't have a residence here, none of the crimes were committed here. And you know that."

"Not the sex trafficking," he acknowledges. "But I've heard things too. Money laundering. Campaign finance violations. And those could be investigated in Virginia."

I don't respond to that. It's off-topic, and a fishing expedition. "The Feds don't have these documents. If they did, there would be no value in the blackmailing efforts with fakes."

"So you know this photo is a fake?"

I nod grimly. "I sure do. I've poured over a lot of photos from Lively's plane. See that bar in the background? That was replaced with an extra chair almost a decade ago. But this photo of Mayfair is newer than that."

"It's not a single image, at least not one that Mayfair has access to," Wilson says. "I ran image comparisons against every photo I could get my hands on, and nothing pinged. It also has a couple of weird pixel spots where it could be doctored."

"A composite image." I think about my conversation with Detective Browning. "If they're this good, it will make it very hard to trust evidence. That benefits chaos agents more than anyone else. And the mission discipline to keep this from exploding—this isn't being outsourced. We're looking at chaos agents who have the capabilities to do all of this in-house. International bank accounts, masking digital trails, and photo manipulation."

Jason points to the photographs. "What if the entire rumored massive document collection that you've heard about is fake? Could these blackmail attempts be an effort to validate the existence of something which does not actually exist?"

I run that scenario through the loose connections I have in my head. "It's possible. A red herring. But we know that Lively took photos—so it makes sense that there are more, a lot more. The red herring theory could be a red herring in itself." I sigh. "But finding it is proving impossible. Whoever does could be leaking the biggest hack of documents since the Panama Papers."

If that person is me, I'm going to call them the Pervert Papers. I keep that part to myself.

We run through the all the facts a few more times, coming at them from different directions, until my stomach rumbles.

Jason immediately offers to order in dinner. He points at Wilson. "You want something?"

"From where? That Filipino place?"

"Yeah."

"Get me my usual."

The deja vu is fucking with my head. And the ordinary office-ness of the whole exchange, when we've just been talking about blackmail and misdirection at the highest levels...it's bizarre.

Jason turns to me. "And you?"

"I'll have one of everything," I quip. "No seriously, I'll have whatever you're having. And maybe whatever Wilson is having too. I haven't eaten since breakfast."

"I hope because you were sleeping." Jason gives me a

look like he doubts that I was, except I was, and I don't need to tell him either way.

I smile sweetly until he leaves. Then I turn back to Wilson. "Can I ask you another question?"

"Shoot."

"Hypothetically, if this stockpile of incriminating evidence is so hard to get our hands on...could we assume it's behind an air-gap protection? On a closed network?"

He gives me an impressed look. "Nice hypothesis. Do you have one in mind?"

"I was just wondering if there's any data in the images that might give us a clue to how they were removed from that system."

"You think maybe the fakes come from the same network? Why not keep the real documents in a secure location and not worry about the fakes?"

"Someone like Mayfair has all the resources in the world to throw at proving something is fake. You have to make it at least a little hard. So just in case...I wonder if there is signature data somewhere."

"The EXIF data was wiped," Wilson said. "One of the first things we looked at. But let's look at the other metada-ta." He right clicks on the image and opens the properties tab. It all looks exactly as one would expect, with no flashing lights that pointed to an evil enterprise having created it.

It was created the day it was emailed to Jeff Mayfair, which doesn't surprise me. The time matches up to the email almost exactly, so the previous metadata was wiped.

It wasn't *actually* created four and a half minutes before being emailed, it was just copied into existence in its new location then.

I frown.

Four and a half minutes.

"Show me the other email. The other image. The times." I trace my finger over the metadata on the screen. Four and a half minutes again. "That's weird, right? And it's not precise, it's a few seconds off. But the files were created, then roughly four and a half minutes later, they were emailed. What if that's how long it takes to transfer the images from one part of a network to another?"

"That's a slow-ass network."

"Dial-up speeds."

Wilson does some quick math on a pad of paper. "Worse."

"What if they're using something like that, a dial-out technology, to create temporary connections across a network?"

He shakes his head. "Yeah, I mean it's possible. But I have another idea. It's possible to use FM frequency signals to cross an air-gap to a closed network. Usually it's a hacking scenario, but what it could be used deliberately."

My eyes light up. "Wait, it can be used to hack into a system?"

"Sure. Easier for an insider to do it than an outsider. But not impossible. There's been some good research about jamming those networks with radio waves, too. How much do you know about closed systems?"

"It's not connected to the internet, so there's no way for hackers to get in. And they can't order takeout."

He laughs.

"I have my priorities straight," I point out.

We're still talking about what those systems look like—including the wild potential of custom storage devices to avoid any USB thumb drive access—when Jason returns.

"Food's here." He hands Wilson a takeout bag. His gaze lingers on me. "Are you guys done? Do you want to eat in my office?"

A flush of heat sweeps through me. "Yeah. Almost, I'll be there in a minute."

Wilson doesn't acknowledge the undercurrent, but I'm sure he caught it. Wilson doesn't miss much. He opens his dinner—a rice bowl with spiced meat, pickled onions, and a couple of lemons on the side—as I flip through my notebook.

"So if there is a database locked away in a closed network like that, what you're saying is, it would take being physically present to copy it, and then I'd need some way to read a custom storage device if we were able to even get to that point."

He shrugs. "Pretty much. But data is all the same. Building a reader would be the easy part. Which is the thing that's always the weak point. Data exists, ergo, data can be copied. Better to have tight op-sec than build a labyrinthian system. Besides, someone can always just take the entire computer. And there are downsides to an air-gapped network, too."

"Like what?"

"The most obvious is that if the servers are destroyed, it's gone. No cloud backup."

I scribble down, *what are the chances a narcissist destroys that kind of record?*

Wilson reads my mind. "That kind of total destruction is always done as a last resort. People like Lively—and you and I both know there are others out there, exactly like him —they don't think they're going to get caught. He didn't think he was going to get caught the second time, even after we took him down once." He grins. "That was very well done on your part."

But it wasn't enough. "He still weaseled out in the end."

"Yeah. They do that."

"They?"

"Motherfucking assholes."

"Amen." I flip the notebook shut. "Thanks for the context."

"Anytime." He picks the lemons off his rice bowl. "I need to remember to tell them to leave these off next time."

I laugh. "More for those of us who love them. I grew up eating them like oranges. Love me some acid on my food. Limes, too. So good."

"Get out of my office," he says fondly. "Jason is waiting for you."

I grin. "I've missed this. Don't tell him I said this, but I am genuinely sorry that I deceived you guys before.

Working here was a genuine joy. You were my friends for real."

"Your secret is safe with me." He winks. "Now get out so I can be a picky eater in peace."

I'm giggling as I arrive in Jason's office.

"Wilson entertained you?"

"Something like that. He was always my fav, you know."

"I'll choose not to be offended by that," Jason murmurs. His desk is spread with takeout containers, and the echo of a time long ago hits me right in the chest.

"You were my secret favorite for other reasons."

"Were?"

"I don't have favorites any more. Life got too complicated for that."

"Fair enough. Sit. Eat."

I dig in. "Wilson's changed. He's softer."

"Becoming a father will do that to a guy, I've heard."

My head swivels to the doorway, to the hallway I just came from, then snaps back to Jason. "He has a kid?"

He nods. "Two of them now. A girl and a baby boy."

"Aww." That makes me happy. "What are their names?"

Jason smirks. "None of your business."

I deserve that. "Okay."

"No, for real. He keeps that secret. We don't know, either."

That honestly doesn't surprise me. "I've missed a lot."

"You haven't been watching?"

How do I explain that I left because I couldn't spy on him? I turned my back, and I meant it. I stayed away for *years*. "No."

His gaze is piercing. Analytical. "There's more to it than that."

"Isn't there always?" I part my lips and tease the corner of my mouth with the tip of my tongue. Wet, slick. Pink. I'm offering him a distraction and we both know it. "Have you interrogated me enough?"

"I thought it was the other way around." His gaze stays locked on my mouth.

Do you want me on my knees?

I would suck him off for the joy of it, but if he thinks I'm offering my mouth to get out of this conversation, that's fine, too.

But he's not done with questions. "Why Melinda?"

I smile. "It's my name."

"Is it?"

"I'm actually not very good at false identities, so I try to keep it simple. Variations on a theme, if you will."

"And Gray..."

"That's made up."

"Any chance you'll share your real last name?"

My smile is a proper grin now. "Nope."

"Just checking."

My phone vibrates in my bag, and I reach down to grab it. But it's not my main phone. It's the burner that I use with Caroline. Fingers shaking, I pick it up.

[14]

JASON

ELLIE'S FACE goes white as she pulls her phone out of her bag.

"What is it?" I'm already out of my chair and around the desk.

"Somebody has Caroline's phone," she whispers.

I shake my head. "Wilson has it."

"Not that one. We use burners to keep some of our conversations off of her work phone. I didn't look to grab hers to bring with us when we came here last night." She gives me a wide-eyed look. "It may already have been taken at that point, but why? And not that the person would know this, but this phone number, *my burner*, is the only one that has any history with hers. Literally, we swap them out regularly. But somebody has it, and they're pretending to be her. *Look.*"

She shows me the screen. The text message on the

creen is from a phone number, not assigned to a contact in
he phone.

555-451-1765: If you want to see Caroline alive again, be prepared to transfer five hundred thousand dollars to a numbered bank account tomorrow morning.

It's a ransom demand. My stomach lurches, and I grab my phone, dialing Deacon.

He answers right away. "What's up?"

"You still with her?"

"Sure am. We're playing Scrabble."

"Can we talk to her for a second?"

There's a fumble, and then Ellie's friend comes on the line. I put her on speaker. "This is she," Caroline says.

Ellie lets out a rough breath. "Hey. Good. Just needed to be sure. Love you."

Caroline sighs. "Same, boo. Stay safe."

"Same." She taps the end call button the screen, then paces across the room. "Okay, what's our next step?"

"Let's go interrupt Wilson's dinner and see if we can triangulate a text message source if we engage. Otherwise, we ignore for now."

"But—" She swallows the protest. "For now?"

"For a hot second. We need to figure out the endgame here. A fake ransom demand is the same game plan as a fake blackmail image. Why?" I leave that question hanging in the air as we hurry to Wilson's office. I text Cole and Tag and tell them to come in, too. "I hope to God everyone is rested. It's going to be a long night."

Ellie gives me a sidelong, skeptical glance. "Did *you* get any sleep?"

I'll sleep when this is over. "I'm fine."

Wilson's happy to set his food aside. "What fucking nonsense is someone playing at?"

"And why would they send it to this phone?" I shake my head. "It doesn't make any sense. We can't track the location from a single text, right?"

Wilson shakes his head. "To start to triangulate a location, I would need to send some silent data requests along with responses. I'd want at least three replies in short succession. The chances of getting that aren't great. But if we can get them to send an image..."

Ellie's hands are shaking. She clenches them together in front of her body. "Do we ask them for a request for proof of life?"

I make a doubting face. "One that they don't have?"

"Maybe they'll doctor it?" She gestures at Jeff Mayfair's dossier, still open on Wilson's screen. "Look at how easy it is in the right hands."

"A good fake takes time. If we ask for proof of life, they'll have to come up with something quickly."

We're still arguing over how to respond when Cole and Tag arrive. We brief them, then Wilson throws his hands in the air. "I dunno. Six of one, half-a-dozen of the other. Who's in favor of asking for proof of life?"

Ellie throws her hand in the air. Cole joins her, and Wilson shrugs, then shoves his hand up, too.

"Three to two," Ellie says triumphantly.

Tag does a slow blink. "I was still thinking."

I huff a sigh. "Fine, we're all in agreement. Reluctantly. I want them to engage back and forth a bit, first."

"Deal." Ellie grabs Wilson's note pad and scratches out a couple of responses. We tweak them to make them as response-prompty as possible, then Wilson types back to the pretend kidnappers, using an app on his computer that clones the phone and ghosts a data ping request beneath the text message.

555-788-2119: I don't have that kind of money available. I can get it, but it will take time.

We all wait. It takes longer than I like for them to reply.

555-451-1765: No stalling. We know what you are capable of. We know who you really are.

Ellie rolls her eyes. "That's more bluster."

"Who knows that you are Caroline's best friend? You, as in, Melinda Gray."

"Nobody," she says immediately and without hesitation. "There is nothing that ties her to me as a reporter."

"Then who else might they think would be at the other end of this text message exchange, if not an infamous journalist?" On Ellie's burner phone, this exchange is the start of the texting history. "How often does she clear her history? What might they see on her phone?"

Ellie chews on her bottom lip. "Our texts are... friendly. No, I guess it's more intimate than that. We're vague about locations and never share anything identifying. Not *intimate* intimate, get your mind out of the gutter, Cole."

He waves his hands in the air. "Whoa. Yeah, no, I don't care what you do with your friends."

I care an absolute fuck ton, but also, not actually my fucking business. I grind my teeth. "So they might mistake you for her lover."

Ellie thinks about it. "Yes. Sure, that's just as likely."

"Do you know who her lover is? Five hundred thousand is a curious ransom amount. It feels specific. Like it's a known amount that might actually be feasible for their target."

Her face pales. "No clue. I wish I did. As far as I know, she's been single for months."

"Any secret affairs? A married partner?"

"Not Caroline's style." She hesitates. "Should we ask her?"

I shake my head. "The less contact we have with Deacon the better. I called him for an immediate proof that this is bullshit. Now, we're on our own."

"Okay, then let's tell them... *if you know who I am...*"

As Ellie dictates, Wilson types.

555-788-2119: If you know who I am, you know it'll

take me time to get the money, but I'll do anything to save her. Please, I'm begging.

The response is immediate.

555-451-1765: You have until noon. Bank details to follow.

"Anything on the data ping?"

"Nothing." Wilson shrugs. "It was worth a shot."

"Then we have nothing to lose. Might as well ask for proof of life, right?" Ellie looks around the room. "Right?"

I nod. "Go for it."

555-788-2119: How do I know you really have her?

No response. We all stand there, holding our breath, but the phone's screen turns off after a minute.

"It'll take them a while," Wilson says. "Let's talk about next steps either way. If they don't reply, and if they do."

"At some point, we'll need to get the FBI involved. I'll let the U.S. Marshals dictate that timeline, based on the security of their protectee, but we don't want to do anything now that will foul up an investigation. My guess is that by morning, we'll want to have Ellie back in her apartment with this phone so they can set up a command center there."

"Oh, no," she objects. "No no. That will draw way too much attention to me and my apartment."

"We'll find you a new place to live after this."

"I like the place I already have!" She shakes her head. "Not that it matters. As soon as this is over, I'm getting on a plane back to California. D.C. is bad for my blood pressure."

The reminder that her return to my life is intensely temporary hits me in the chest like a sledgehammer. Depending on what the Feds want to do with her and Caroline, tonight could be the last time I see her.

And I wouldn't put it past Ellie to disappear again, this time for good.

"I'm going to put on some coffee," I say abruptly.

Ellie tries to catch my stony gaze as I stalk out of Wilson's office, but I ignore the effort. I need a minute to myself.

[15]

MELINDA

I WATCH JASON STORM OFF, and when I glance back at the other guys, they suddenly busy themselves.

"I'm going to check my messages," Cole says.

Tag nods. "Yeah. Ditto. Gotta call a guy back about a thing."

Which leaves me and Wilson alone in his office, and I'm between him and the door.

"I guess that makes me the messenger," he says blandly.

"No message required." I point to the screen. "Let's get back to work."

He turns off his monitors. "Nope."

I open my mouth to protest, then stop myself. They have a right to give me shit for deceiving them. "Okay. Hit me."

"You broke his heart."

I do a double take. "What? No."

"Seriously. He moped around for months after you disappeared."

"It wasn't like that."

"It was for him. And it's not for me to tell you more than that, but you reappearing—and turning out to be another power player on the scene, in a way—has really done a number on him."

"He's stronger than that." We both are. That's how I knew we could have an affair all those years ago.

"It's not about strong or not." Wilson looks at me steadily. "I have a family now."

"Jason told me." I give him an earnest, warm smile. "I'm thrilled for you. Honestly."

"I would kill for my kids. For my wife. Destroy whole kingdoms. And if they were taken from me, I would be an empty shell of a man. There is no strength in the world that can make up for that loss."

"I'm not that to him," I whisper.

"Maybe not. But you could have been."

"That wasn't real."

His mouth twists in a grimace. "Yes. We're very aware of that."

Fuck me. "I'll go and talk to him. You've got it all wrong."

Wilson shrugs. "Maybe."

I spin on my heel and go in search of Jason, and coffee, and answers. He's not in the kitchenette, where a pot of coffee is brewing. I go next to his office, but he's not there, either.

I loop back to Wilson's office. "He may have headed out."

"The roof, maybe." He taps into their surveillance system. It's dark up there, with lots of shadows, but the boss man can be made out just fine. "Yep."

He hands me a keycard. "Do you remember how to get up there?"

"Yeah."

"He really was changed after you left."

I shake my head. "That started before I went. Cole changed him." It's why I... I swallow back that thought.

"No. You did it, too. You were a ray of sunshine in his darkness."

"That wasn't really me."

"I dunno about that."

"I'm no Little Miss Sunshine."

"Hope comes in a lot of different packages, Ellie."

I want to correct them every time they use my nickname. But I like it, too, and I don't want to dwell too long on *that* idea, so I take the stairs two at a time and burst out into the warm night air just as Jason turns around.

"Do we have a photo?"

"Not yet." The door shuts behind me, and we're alone. The roof is built up along the edges, and has a bunch of nooks and crannies with covered shelter spots, so it feels private up here even with the street noise below. "Wilson seems to think we should hash out the past."

"And what does Melinda Gray think?"

"There are more important things going on right now."

"I'm fully aware that you wouldn't be here if you could help it." He turns and looks south toward the Washington Monument. "I'm not having any trouble focusing on the real issues at hand, I assure you."

"I have no doubt. You're a kingmaker."

"Do you believe that?"

I move closer to him. "As much as anyone can be. Nobody controls this game, though."

"That's the problem, isn't it?" He glances sideways at me. "There are people who think they do. But we're all pawns."

I nod. "Even the people who think they pull the strings... We're all at the mercy of everyone else."

His mouth quirks. "That's the social experiment, isn't it? We all lift each other up?"

"Well, if you insist on putting a positive spin on it." I move past him, sliding into the shadows beneath an overhang. I'm pretty sure Wilson can't see me here, and even if he can, he'll turn off the monitor and find something else to do. I undo my belt and the silk panels of my dress slide against my body, falling open.

Jason's gaze drops to my breasts, lingering there long enough for my nipples to harden under his appraisal, then he rakes his hot inspection lower. To my belly and the shadow between my legs.

"You don't know what you're doing."

"Really?" I smirk. "I think I do. It's time you stop underestimating me."

He moves against me, pushing me deeper into the

shadow. His fingers tangle in my hair, holding me still as he crushes his mouth against mine. Hard, ruthless, demanding.

When he pulls away, his grip tightens. "How do you see this going? You think I'm going to fuck you, and we'll forget the rest of the conversation we should have had?"

"If only it were that easy." I lick my lips, wet still from the savaging of his kiss. "I didn't come up here to distract you."

"That's a shame. I could use a distraction right now." He nips at my jaw. "We both could. Talking is overrated." His devouring mouth moves to my neck, his breath hot against my ear. "I know we don't have long, Ellie. We don't need to hash anything out. It's fine."

It's not, really, but talking won't make it any better.

But before we get further than his mouth on my breasts, his phone goes off.

He digs it out. "There's a response. They've sent a photo."

I tug my dress back together and smooth down my hair.

Jason straightens my belt, then catches my chin between his thumb and forefinger. "Hey. Whatever the photo looks like...it's not real."

"I know."

"And we'll continue this later."

"Yeah."

He frowns.

"What?"

"What are you running from?"

"Nothing," I say lightly.

He catches me around the waist and tugs me close again. "Liar."

"Takes one to know one." I kiss him, at first to shut him up, then I keep going because it feels good. A spontaneous sweetness that takes us both by surprise. But fuck it, if the world is going to end, I'm going to have the taste of him on my lips when it does. "Maybe everything. I don't know."

He takes my hand in his and pulls me to the stairwell. "Listen, I don't want you to be alone tonight. Come back to my place."

I shake my head. "No."

He tries to protest, but I cut him off. "You can come to mine, though. If you want."

One more night together. A few more moments that will have to last us a lifetime.

[16]

JASON

THE PHOTO IS DAMN CONVINCING.

Wilson's already running it through image comparison searches when we skid to a halt in his office doorway, and it repeats on three different screens.

Ellie gasps audibly. "I know," she growls. "It's not real, but that fucker."

"We have a data ping, too. The image was sent from New York City."

"Not D.C.?" Ellie scoots in closer to the screen. "That phone took quite a trip today."

"Or it's a deliberate misdirection," Wilson warns her.

"Mmm. Good point." She snaps her fingers as she examines the image properties. "Hey, is that... That's not a coincidence," she whispers to Wilson. "Right?"

"Four and a half minutes. I don't think it's a coincidence at all."

"What are you two talking about?" I bark the question

at them.

"We've figured out a bit of data on the images that could serve as a digital signature," Wilson says. "A time gap between two pieces of data on the file. There's no reason for it to be consistent across multiple images from different sources, so..."

Ellie straightens up, her face set in a grim expression. "We're maybe dealing with a single bad actor. Whoever tried to blackmail Jeff Mayfair is also pretending to have Caroline."

"Who would benefit from that?" I can't make sense of it. "There's nothing that ties the two cases together."

"It's a post-truth world. Nothing matters if everything is suspect. Maybe the ransom isn't the goal. Maybe the confusion and doubt is the goal." Ellie points in the general direction of the street. "Maybe someone has a camera trained on the entrance to your building. They saw Caroline approach, obviously in distress, greeted by Cole—who also brought in Jeff Mayfair, right?"

Cole frowns. "But then they would know that we have her and she's safe?"

"Right. Which immediately means these text messages are not what they seem, so we go looking for a different explanation." Ellie's storming ahead, the words tripping out of her mouth she's talking so fast, and I'm stuck on the idea of our offices being under surveillance.

I just had her naked on the roof. Were we in shadows the whole time? What if I had fucked her up there? My vision goes a furious shade of red.

But my would-be lover is still focused on a complicated theory I've now lost half the train of thought on. Fuck.

She pops her hands on her hips. "All of us, right now, are looking in the wrong spot...or maybe from the wrong angle."

Cole is nodding along with her. "Right. Who benefits from that?"

Nobody.

The truth is, there's no benefit in that kind of toxic malevolence. If Ellie's right, and someone is trying to mind-fuck us, it's because they've gone past the point of no return. Or, even worse, they've decided this is the endgame for them.

What stops madmen from wreaking destruction at every turn? The fear that it might not be *enough* damage. They wait, biding their time for the right opportunity, and enjoying life in the meantime—because life as you know it comes to a screeching halt once you rain fire down on others. It's the same for despots and dictators, for serial killers and cultists.

The final showdown is always bloody, brutal, and inevitably ends in failure, because the good guys outnumber the bad guys.

But evil people start out more quietly than that. They find subtle ways to hurt others. Privately at first. Then, inch by inch, they creep into public view. Normalizing abuse of those around them, converting victims into accomplices, witnesses into apologists. And for a long time, we don't even realize we're a part of the destruction.

There is no corner of the world where power has not been corrupted, where power has not *corrupted* those who have it.

Including me and my firm.

If someone is targeting us, it's the next step in a plan. They're someone who has had contact with us in the past. A client or a target. I look at my colleagues and see equally furious expressions on their faces. "Who has a score to settle with us?"

The shorter answer may be, who doesn't.

"I'll write an algorithm to make some predictions," Wilson says. "It'll take the better part of the night to give us some potential leads. Everyone should try to get some sleep."

I point to the screen. "We're not replying to this, right?"

Ellie flips her middle finger in the direction of the photo. "Nope. Thanks for the data, but we're done with this nonsense."

Great. "All right. I'll make contact with the marshals and we'll reconvene here at six tomorrow morning."

We shower together.

We don't talk.

There's a pulsing awareness as we dry off that we're about to tumble into her bed, about to fuck ourselves into a state of exhaustion, and in the morning, something is going to happen.

A raid, if we're lucky. An arrest, God willing.

And then she'll disappear.

Wilson thinks we should hash out the past? There's no time for that. How does one go back in time that far and unpack all the feelings one stumbled into then, in any kind of rational way? It would get messy. Ugly. Mean.

Even that little thought spikes an irrational, unacceptable anger inside me. I cannot hate this woman and fuck her at the same time. That's not who I am.

From the moment she kissed me, I let all those old feelings go.

We make choices, and this is mine.

Ellie. Here. Now.

I seduce her in the shower. Lingering strokes, firm pressure. Squeezes all over. The side of her neck, the tight trap leading to her shoulder. Her sensitive spots on her sides, the tops of her thighs, then down her legs.

Back up again, this time with my mouth.

When we climb out, I dry her off, then tangle my hands in her hair, holding her head as I bring our mouths together. Her lips fit perfectly against mine, parting for me.

I explore her entire body with careful thoroughness, holding back the beast inside of me that wants to just gorge itself on the taste of her pussy.

It's been too long.

But tonight, either because of fatigue or sympathy or both, Ellie's gone soft for me, and I want to match that for her. Show her that the man, when stripped out of the suit, is just as human as the rest.

Or at least I hope I am. It's been far too long since I've even tried.

I don't put my mouth to her pussy until she's begging for it, and I lick her through two orgasms before I slide into her tightness.

When I finish, her name on my lips, she gets rid of the condom and tucks me into bed.

Her hand drifts across my chest, warm and soft, and my eyelids drift shut. I'm not ready for what tomorrow is going to bring. It's all too close, too raw, and far too dangerous for my liking. We both need our rest, but I'm terrified that when I wake up, she'll be gone.

I want to ask her again what she's running from, but I don't want another brush off. She's set that boundary. It's none of my business. I push my face into the soft curve of her neck and let sleep wash over me.

————

It's still dark when I sit straight up, still waking even as I try to get out of the unfamiliar bed.

"Hey, hey." Ellie catches me by the wrist. "You okay?"

"Washroom," I mutter, stumbling in the direction of the sink. I need cold water on my face. My bad dream is already receding, I can't get a handle on it, but whatever it was, I don't want to go back to it.

After I piss, I open the door to find her making coffee with a simple pour over drip filter.

"I didn't mean to wake us both up," I say, dropping a

kiss on her bare shoulder. Pretending, if only for my own selfish reasons, that this is just a regular early morning and not the last time we might be alone. And after checking my phone, I realize our time together has to be cut even shorter than I'd like.

"I had that long nap yesterday. And we got a solid six. That's more than I usually get."

I frown. "Why?"

"Why do forty percent of grown-ass adults struggle with getting enough sleep?" She shrugs. "Life is complicated, my day job haunts my dreams, and I drink too much caffeine around the clock."

"At least you are aware of the issue," I say dryly.

She snorts. "Is that a yes to caffeine?"

"That's a hell yes."

She hands me a cup. "What haunts your dreams?"

"Damned if I know. I suppress that shit like a pro." I breathe in the scent of the black coffee and watch as she makes herself a mug. "Listen, it's actually good that I woke up this early. I need to run a quick errand before we meet the others at the office."

Her eyebrow curves up. "An errand? So early?"

"It's not related to this."

"Okay. I'll see you there."

"I'll come back and get you."

She shakes her head. "I'll meet you there. I can take care of myself."

I don't like that at all. "Stay safe."

She gives me a tight smile. "You, too."

[17]

MELINDA

I'M VERY TEMPTED to follow Jason to his mysterious five o'clock in the morning errand. But I'm also glad he's gone, so I can run an errand of my own before rendezvousing at his office.

Keeping secrets is messy at the best of times, and this is not the best of times.

"There's a safe deposit box with your name on it."

To any eavesdropping observer, that would probably suggest Caroline had a box at a bank, and put my name on it as a backup.

But that's not what she meant.

And I know she's not dead, but the way this situation is escalating quickly, I may not get another chance alone to go and see what she secreted away in her locker at the gym.

I pull out the box of wigs I keep under my bed and grab a long-haired blonde one that will allow me to approximate Caroline for the gym staff. An oversized pair of sunglasses and her gym access card from her wallet, which I kept, is all I need.

Heading downstairs, I get my motorbike out of the storage unit, tighten my sling bag so it's snug against my body, and start the ignition.

It's a short drive to the gym. I pop ear buds in and crank music so nobody will try to talk to me. Then I swipe Caroline's card through the reader, push through the gate, and head straight to the change room.

Her card also opens her locker. Inside is a gym bag, which I rifle through, but it contains nothing of interest. Workout clothes, shoes, hair elastics, condoms.

I feel around the sides of the locker, but it doesn't look like she modified it in any way. No false ceiling, nothing gives way.

Maybe I misunderstood the hint. Maybe she really does have a safety—

My brain skips back over the items I had just seen.

Condoms.

They're regular latex condoms, and Caroline is allergic to latex. I grab the box and pull the condoms out. It's a full box, and the first few packs are exactly as I'd expect to find them. But the last strip is firmer to the touch—almost as if there's something inside them. My bet is memory cards.

I don't bother confirming that hunch right now. I put everything back, shove the altered condom strip in my sling bag, and head back to my bike.

But as soon as I'm back on the street, I get a bad feeling—like I'm being watched. I'm two miles from Jason's office.

It's early still, traffic is light. I make a judgement call, trust my skills on the road. I can make it.

Sure enough, as I zip into the flow of cars, I see a black sedan pull out behind me. They keep pace, not closing the gap.

There's a chance this is the good guys, so to speak— federal agents keeping an eye on me from a distance.

I don't like that, but I don't hate it.

It's preferable to the alternative, which is that the sedan is full of baddies with guns, and I'm riding high on my bike with zero bulletproof glass around me.

Slowly, I pick up speed. Getting pulled over for riding a crotch rocket too fast right now would be a complication I don't need.

There's a stale green light ahead, and I really don't want to get caught at a red, so I zoom forward. The sedan follows, closing the gap now, and just as we reach the inter-section, a truck turns right off the cross street, directly into my lane.

That's no coincidence, not the way the sedan is jamming up behind me. I don't want to get boxed in, either. I take a split-second look in the mirror, swing to the right and grab the front brake, using the momentum of my body to shuffle the bike in a 180 turn so now I'm facing the surprised driver of the sedan previously behind me.

There's someone in the passenger seat, too.

Two men. Beefy. Ex-military. Not in suits, nothing says FBI about them.

Mercenaries is my bet, and holy fuck, no thank you.

So long, assholes.

I accelerate and take off the wrong way through traffic.

Barely stopping at the next block, I take a hard right and cut a terrifying path through oncoming traffic before sliding into a stream of cars going the right direction. I need to get underground and fast.

My apartment is closer than Jason's office, so I zoom home. Pulse racing, I swipe my fob that opens the garage door.

The seconds it takes to lift feel like hours.

I race down the ramp, taking the curve faster than is safe, and skid to a stop in front of my storage unit. I don't know if the bike has been tagged by the people following me, so I might have no time at all here before I've got company again.

Taking the stairs, I bolt upstairs and dump my sling bag into a larger backpack. I add my laptop to it and a couple of important pieces from the safe—including my passport.

I don't know if it's safer to try to hop on transit, or catch a cab, or go out my back window and take my chances crossing the grounds of the Naval Observatory.

I decide to head outside and get on a bus or in a cab, whichever comes along first—but when I get to the ground floor, I see one of the goons from the car prowling around the lobby.

He's gotta be six feet, nine inches and three hundred pounds. I'm a good fighter, but against this guy it's like a two-against-one match.

Reversing course, I sprint back up to the second floor

and take the back stairs instead, bursting out into the side alley—and headlong into a solid wall of muscle.

Before I can scream, a hand clamps over my mouth and I'm wrenched around, my backpack giving whoever has grabbed me a good wallop as they drag me backwards.

The next thing I see is Jason's stony face, scowling at me as he shoves me into the passenger seat of his car.

[18]

JASON

By the time I get around to the driver's side, Ellie has her backpack off and unzipped. My heart stops for a second when I see she has a Glock in her hand, but she's not pointing it at me.

Small miracle.

I shove the car into first gear and reverse out of the alley, barely coming to a stop before I take off. As the car rights itself, I glance across at her. "Why do you have a gun?"

"Things got a bit messy this morning."

I don't like the way she says that. What the fuck does *messy* mean? "Put that away. Guns are dangerous."

She stares at me incredulously.

"They are," I point out blandly, trying to maintain some control over the conversation.

"Jesus, Jason, now is not the time to be ethical." She

shoves the Glock at me. "You can have this one. I have another in here."

Great, she has an entire arsenal. That doesn't make any sense at all. "Why?"

"Seriously, someone tried to kidnap me and you're asking questions?"

"Yes. Top of the list is, why did someone try to kidnap you?"

She doesn't answer that directly. "How did you find me?"

"At your apartment? Where you live?"

"Coming out the side door."

"I didn't like the look of those guys in the front. I'm taking it they're the potential kidnappers?"

"This isn't funny."

"I'm definitely not laughing." I hold up my hand as I place a call to Wilson. "We're five minutes out. Might be coming in hot."

"For real?"

"Yeah. Unfortunately."

"All right. Cole and Tag will be on the lookout."

I end the call. "We'll be safe at the office. What do I need to know before we get there?"

She's looking out the back window. "I dunno."

"All right. What don't I know?"

"I can't properly answer that question right now."

"But you can give me a gun."

"It's complicated."

"Un-fucking-complicate it, then."

"You can't get mad."

That's a guarantee that whatever it is will infuriate me. "Okay."

"Jason."

"I will contain my reaction. Because from where I stand, it looks like you're the target in all of this. Someone used Jeff Mayfair to go to me, knowing that was your story, that we would be drawn together, and then they escalated shit fast. Your best friend got attacked. You got the ransom demand. It's not random at all, Ellie. You are the common denominator."

She drags in a ragged breath. "Yeah. I've come to the same conclusion this morning."

"What happened?"

"I went to pick something up. Something of Caroline's."

"More secrets?"

"I don't even know what it is. I just had a hunch that she might have stashed some computer files at her gym. I haven't read them yet. I was followed from there. Two cars, a black sedan. An Audi." She pauses, then rhymes off a license plate.

I voice text that to Wilson.

"And a truck, but honestly, I didn't make out any details. The guys in the Audi looked like mercenaries. So yeah, it's starting to click in... Because a few months ago, I got wind of a potential story. And keep in mind, a lot of what I'm about to say, I'm just figuring out now, in hindsight. I think maybe as soon as I started poking around, a misdirection campaign began. Of course, I didn't know that at the time. The person responsible for it didn't want me to know about those seeds they were sowing. They purposefully blackmailed people who would either pay out, or ignore it. Nobody who would go to the police. Really top-level profiling shit, that. Very impressive. But I'm getting ahead of myself. Your client is one of those targets, as you guessed. But I don't know that he wanted you involved. I think that's...I dunno. I'm not sure about that part. My own guess was that he assumed Mayfair would fall into the *ignore it* category. He almost certainly did not expect him to go to you, and treat this as a real crisis that required a proper response."

"Huh." I take the next turn faster than the one before. "Yeah, that was bad luck. Mayfair has had all of his lovers sign NDAs, and he got spooked, but not enough to feel guilty."

"Oh." She chews on her lower lip, as if mentally adding that to the story file. "Fascinating."

"I think I'm following. So you were on this story when you came here."

"Caroline had alluded to it being good for me to spend some time in D.C. as things were going down. She's deep into a case she can't talk about, but...I might want to be here instead of on the west coast. I don't need to be told twice when there's a story about to break open. At that point, I thought they weren't related."

"And then Caroline was attacked."

Ellie doesn't take the prompt. She makes a thinking noise.

"Ellie."

Still silence.

I punch my hand against the steering wheel. "You knew, didn't you? You knew that you were the target, and you still went out alone."

"I didn't know for sure. I had my suspicion, sure, because what other tie could there be? Don't you think I'm *gutted* that she was assaulted? I will live with that for the rest of my fucking life."

I grind my teeth. "Sorry."

"Yeah, you should be." She sighs. "I'm sorry I went out alone."

"We both need to trust each other a touch more." I whip the car into our parking garage, which has Cole and Tag outside it standing guard.

It doesn't seem like we were followed, which is a minor victory, but the reprieve won't last long.

I park close to the elevator, and just as I turn the car off, my phone lights up in its holder on my dashboard.

Beside me, Ellie's phone goes off, too.

It's a text message from Caroline's burner phone.

555-451-1765: You aren't playing my game. So I'm changing the rules.

[19]

MELINDA

THE TEXT MESSAGE has photos attached to it. A lot of
them. They're scans of pages from a file that I recognize,
and at the top is a name. My name, my real name, with not
very much redacted on each page.

Jason and I both get out of the car at the same time,
squaring off. He still has my Glock and I have my Sig. How
the fuck did it get to this?

He glares at me. Before he can say anything, Wilson
bursts through the door from the stairwell, running toward
us at full speed.

"She's CIA," Wilson spits.

"Settle down," I say as calmly as I can muster. "You
didn't need to rush down here. You're being played.
Obviously."

Wilson doesn't take his eyes off me, but his tone shifts
as he addresses Jason. "You can't trust her."

"I don't," Jason says evenly, and something in my chest shifts.

Back to feeling hollow, I guess. I swallow hard. It's fine. I lift my voice to a definitely-not-affected-by-that note. "That makes two of us."

He laughs humorlessly. "Now is not the time, Melinda."

"So we're back to given names again?"

"I don't know." He circles around so he's standing beside Wilson, and that hollow feeling gapes wider. In his hand is a weapon I just gave him, like a fucking fool. "Tell me who you are."

"You *know* who I am. I'm a journalist. I write as Melinda Gray. That's not a lie."

Wilson's lips are so tense, they're white. "You aren't from Chicago."

I hesitate.

Jason swears under his breath.

"No," I whisper. "I'm not."

"Where are you from?"

"What on earth does it matter?"

"Why are you back in D.C.?"

"I've already told you." I glance at the Glock. "Can you put that away?"

"Or what?"

I give them a level look. "If you think I'm CIA, you can answer that one for yourselves. Do you really want this to end in a shootout beneath your offices?"

Jason swears again.

Slow footsteps approach.

"She's armed," Jason calls out.

Cole grunts. "So are we."

I pivot just enough to include him in my arc. "Oh great, now it's a party. I mean, we can do this, but we're doing it without the threat of someone losing an eye. Got it?" I glare at Cole first, betting that Jason is the less likely to shoot me. *Sure hope so.* "Gun down."

Cole doesn't move. "You first."

I don't move either.

Jason growls at me, but gestures for Cole to relax. "Listen to her. This is obviously meant to get all of our backs up, and it worked. Let's go upstairs."

Wilson protests.

I ignore the sharp pain in my chest at realizing just how easily I was made the bad guy here.

"All of us," Jason repeats. "Upstairs. Ellie, after you."

"Oh no," I drawl. "After you. I insist."

They file onto the elevator, all except Cole, who insists on taking the stairs.

Heart in my throat, I join them in the elevator. Tag swipes his card, and up we go.

We all go into the boardroom, and I reluctantly set my Sig on the sideboard. Jason does the same with my Glock.

Cole refuses to disarm himself, but at least puts his pistol back in the holster he'd put on when we were "coming in hot". Ten minutes ago, when I was still on their team and Jason was doing his utmost to protect me.

"Facts as I see them," Jason starts. "This morning, Ellie

and I both independently came to the same conclusion that she is most likely the target of the bad actor in all of this."

At least he doesn't see me *as* the bad actor, which is a relief.

"Last night," he continues. "When I said, who would want to be out to get us...I should have asked, who would want to get Ellie. So..." He glances at his phone. "Melinda Boyko? Care to start listing your enemies?"

Relief is short-lived.

"Those page scans are a distraction," I repeat. "I am a journalist."

Jason kicks the chair beside him. "A lie of omission is still a filthy fucking lie, *Melinda*. Who the hell were you *before* you were a journalist?"

I take a deep breath. "I worked in the foreign service for a few years. That's how I met Caroline."

"Is that the first honest thing you've ever said to me?"

No. The first honest thing I ever said to him was way back when he thought I was his receptionist, and he fucked me in secret in the kitchenette whenever he had the chance. When I told him I needed him no matter how reckless, no matter how foolish it might be.

I needed him then, anyway. I don't need him now. I can't need him now.

I lift my jaw and glare at him.

"And when you worked in the foreign service? Were you trained by the CIA?"

"Yes."

"Why did you leave the foreign service? That's good cover."

"They don't like loudmouths." I shrug. "I used the Dissent Channel one too many times."

"You used the Dissent Channel." He prowls toward me. "Spoke truth to power. That's quite brave."

I laugh. That's such an idealized way to look at it, and I didn't expect that kind of naivety from Jason. "Tell that to my career."

"You were fired?"

"Encouraged to resign. There was no upward momentum for me."

"How old were you?"

"Twenty-seven."

He pins me to the wall, and I force myself to keep breathing. I only have one good play here, and it's convincing him I'm not the enemy. "How the fuck old are you now?"

I may not be the enemy, but I'm not a great sport about demands. "It's rude to ask a lady her age."

"You are no fucking lady."

"Are you trying to figure out how long it took for me to leave the foreign service and reinvent myself as a journalist looking for a story from behind your reception desk?"

"Yes."

"You won't like the answer."

His eyes glitter as he waits me out. I hold his gaze. We have so much history. But the reason I met him will forever be tainted if he finds out the truth, and I'm not sure I can bear that.

"Everyone get out," he growls. "I think what Ms. Whatever Her Name Is Here has to say, I think it's for my ears alone."

It's a testament to their bond that the other men don't question him. As one, they get up and leave.

But if I thought that it would be easier once we're alone, I was mistaken. I don't know what I thought. I'm having trouble keeping all my emotions in check right now. "Jason," I whisper.

"Shut up." He lets go of me and steps back. "I don't like any of this. I don't like that you lie as easily as you breathe. I don't like that I still want you, no matter how many times you dart away from the truth, *Melinda*."

"Why do you say my name like that?"

"Because I should have known sooner than I did that something wasn't on the up and up with you. It was too easy, the way you wormed your way back into my firm."

"I didn't know where else to go," I hiss at him. "And you know it."

"Lie to me again, Melinda. Lie to my face."

"I hate you."

He kisses me, hard, his mouth a crushing press against mine.

A sob rips from my chest, and he catches my face in his hands.

"What are you scared of?"

"You." I spit the word at him.

He doesn't blink. "Is that supposed to hurt?"

I shrug.

"Because I think you are scared right now. I think *I* scare you, and that means we're finally getting somewhere close to the truth. And that will never slice me as deep as all the lies you've told me with ease."

"I can't tell you who is behind this. You won't believe me. I need to show you."

"I might believe you."

I shake my head. "You said it yourself downstairs. You don't trust me."

"How can I? I don't know you." His jaw clenches. "But I want to trust you. I'm listening."

My mind races. How can I show him what I think I know? "I went to Harvard. I was a scholarship kid, very smart. Too smart. I worked at the Crimson and broke a couple of good stories, but then I wanted to write a story that got killed. And that was my first experience with learning just how powerful money is, and what it can shut down."

"What was the story that got killed?"

"It's weird, you know. On one hand, it's a college experience like any other. Okay, not quite like any other, and I knew that. But on the other hand...sometimes you find out that a classmate's relative funded the overthrow of a government of a country that you have other classmates from. It's fucked up. You see that intense difference in the absolute upper classes right up close in technicolor."

"What country?"

I tell him, and his eyes go wide. "You tried to write about the financier of a revolution?"

"Kind of foreshadowed how my career in the foreign service would go. Because the grandchildren of billionaires either actively work to never be a billionaire themselves, or they think they can overthrow governments for sport. There is no in between. It's hereditary toxic bullshit."

Jason frowns. "I feel like you're leading me somewhere with this."

I try to swallow and I can't, my throat is too dry.

"You're the grandchild of a billionaire," I say weakly.

"And I have no interest in being one myself." His frown gets darker. "What is your point?"

I can't say it.

The darkness in his glower gathers into a full-force gale. "Ellie, what are you saying?"

"Mack," I whisper. "It's Mack."

MELINDA

THE SHOCK on his face sucks all the air out of the room.

He didn't see it. He never saw it, and I'm the one who had to tell him.

"My brother?" His voice cracks and goes up at the end, and I see the little boy inside who worshiped the older brother, the rightful heir, who never really had time for little Jason. Product of a second marriage that didn't last all that long.

The first time I met Mack Evans, at Harvard, I knew he was evil. I was an undergrad. He was an alumnus brought in as part of the CIA's recruitment strategy, although I didn't know it then.

When I found out he'd given seed money to the Horus Group, I knew what my first investigation would be. I had to get inside this organization and expose it for the rot it had to contain.

Instead, I found broken men at a crossroads—and just

as I was prepared to reveal who they were, they chose a better path.

And I fell in love.

The second time I met Mack Evans, I thought he didn't recognize me.

Five years later, I'm realizing I was too naïve for this world.

"He knew who I was," I say, as gently as I could. "He brought me into the CIA. So when he saw me here...in hindsight, he knew."

"I don't understand."

"He was an associate of Gerome Lively."

"No."

"Yes. It will all come out, one way or another." I hope so, anyway. Mack's a loose cannon now. It's possible he's going to try to take me down with him. But I'm not the only one who knows about the incriminating documents Lively stored—and I am more convinced than ever that Mack is the one who inherited that stash. "And he wants the PRISM council seat."

Jason shakes his head. "No. He's...he's..."

I grimace. "Angling for a role in this President's administration? A sinking ship? Does that sound right to you?"

"Fuck."

"It doesn't sound right because it's not right. It's spin, designed to cover up his real power move. Another four years, and he's going to be running for President. And you don't know that because he keeps you in the dark."

"And you, a journalist who has hid on the west coast for five years, knows this...how, exactly?"

I swallow hard. "I have a source. One very close to international intelligence agencies. Canada is going to call for the United Nations to form a criminal tribunal to investigate PRISM. Mack is one of the targets of that investigation."

Jason doesn't move. His hands ball up into fists at his side, his knuckles turning white. "How do you know?"

"Because I know."

"Canada is an active participant in PRISM's leadership summit. Every year, consistently. This year the Prime Minister's principal secretary will attend—"

"No." I shake my head. "He'll go to New York at the last minute. The resolution will pass while those who would object are distracted."

"Jesus."

"I'm not lying to you."

"I want to believe you." But he doesn't yet. Fair is fair. It's going to take some time to sink in. He stands there for a long time, the silence pulsing between us. Finally, his shoulders sag. "How long have you known?"

"Since before I met you."

"He was always the target." Jason's jaw flexes hard, his lips white with tension. "And I was a means to the end."

"Yes." I owe him the truth, however brutal it may be.

"So what happened? Why no great takedown?"

"It's easier said than done." I pause. "And you were

trying. I thought you all might actually get somewhere. But they're more powerful than we ever will be."

"And I was just a pawn in their game."

"We're all pawns," I say as gently as possible. "There is no such thing as a good billionaire, Jason. Not even when they're related to you by blood."

"Blood means nothing," he growls, a rough, angry burst of three words that feel like an entire saga sharpened to a point.

"You have something more important than blood bonds. You have real brothers here." I gesture to the empty hallway behind us. The men who left us alone without question. "They trust you. They will help you here."

"I don't know what to do with this." His voice has lost its rough edge now. He sounds hollow. Rung out.

"I'm sorry."

"You should have told me sooner."

"Would you have believed me? I don't think anyone in the USINT community believes this yet. There's a real rift in the Five Eyes Alliance, Jason. And it's not like I've known all of this for very long myself."

"Your source—is it the Canadian guy?"

"I can't reveal my sources. Not even to you."

"He didn't like me. Mack set up my sit down with him." Jason laughs, and it's so hard and brittle it hurts my ears. "Fucking douchebag. Fucking asshole motherfucker. Fuck—" He stops and looks at me. "You don't think US intelligence is taking this seriously?"

"Not enough to publish it as a story, but...that's what

the rumors are, yeah."

He grabs me by the shoulders. "This conversation isn't over."

"I—"

He crushes his mouth to mine. "I love you, you filthy liar. I love you when I don't even know who you are. I love you when you hate me. I love you when I hate myself. I have to—I have to try to fix this—but I want you to be safe and sound when I get back."

My mouth falls open as he darts into the hallway, yelling for Wilson. They all come running. No no no, I need time to stop while Jason explains to me what the hell he means by saying all of *that* and then turning on his heel and leaving.

"I don't have time to explain everything. Who can come with me to the White House? Tag? You think Kendra can join us? We just need to get to someone on the National Security Council."

"On it." Tag pulls out his phone.

"Wilson, Ellie can explain why, but just know, I do believe her. I trust her. We need to pull Mack's chain. Shut down whatever you can."

"Mack? Your brother?" Wilson doesn't blink. "Got it."

"Cole..." Jason grabs his best friend and points at me. "Sit on her."

"I'm not going anywhere," I protest.

"That is exactly what you would say right before you tried to duck out and save the world all on your lonesome. Stay where he can see you."

[21]

JASON

KENDRA BROWNING DOESN'T ASK a single question about why I'm asking her for this introduction. She's waiting outside the White House with a female Lieutenant-Colonel who seems to immediately recognize Tag and understand the complicated relationship between the divorced couple.

"Kendra says I can trust you," the Air Force officer says as we take a walk, Kendra and Tag falling in behind us. "I don't have a lot of time. I need to be back for a briefing in an hour."

"Any chance you'll be doing that in a room that's not quite round?"

"No comment."

"I'll cut right to the point, then. I know about the schism in the Five Eyes Alliance. I learned about it from a reporter, who got it from another country. You don't have an internal leak. But you do have an internal fight about whether to take this to the Commander-in-Chief, and I'm here to help you get it on his agenda."

"Even if we could get it past his Chief of Staff, POTUS doesn't like the international community saying anything about American businesses."

"Lieutenant-Colonel, do you believe you have a full understanding of the global reach of PRISM?"

"Yes, I believe I do."

"You're wrong. And I say that with full respect for your experience and your rank and your uniform. I have reason to believe that Mack Evans is about to join the PRISM high council, and fundamentally change our democracy in the process. And most people won't realize until it's too late."

"Mr. Evans...your brother is not on any intelligence reports as a candidate..."

"Is there any intelligence reports that he was a close associate of Gerome Lively?"

She stops walking. "No."

"Then please believe me when I tell you, there is much that you don't know about PRISM. But if we can go inside, I'll show you what I know."

In the short span of time it took for Tag and I to get over to the White House, Ellie and Wilson were able to find me enough proof. It's hardly comprehensive, but it's a start.

"I'm not sure if I can get you on the visitor's list..."

Wilson's taken care of that. "I think it'll be fine."

———

An hour later, I've done my best—officially. The NSC staff heard me out and took a detailed report. Then someone from the Chief of Staff's office came in, some weasel-looking shithead who probably graduated straight from a Vegas casino to the West Wing, because that's how Victor Best rolls, and told them the intelligence briefing would be paper-only today.

Victor Best doesn't read anything longer than a room service menu.

It's a brick wall.

I excuse myself and head for the exit. The long way, of course, taking me as close to the Oval Office as visitors can get, which isn't that close, but is close enough that when the notoriously antsy POTUS roams through the halls, I manage to get in front of him.

This was not exactly my plan A. But it will certainly do as a plan B.

"Nice to see you again, sir." The words should stick in my throat like the disingenuous bullshit they are, but they come out smooth as silk. I'm good at this.

Best eyes me up, gives me the once over, and I know exactly what he's thinking, because we have met before. Not that he'll admit it.

"Remind me of your name, young man."

I have met the President of the United States of America at least twice before, and this conversation goes exactly the same way each time. "Jason Evans, sir. Former special warfare operator. You were a great help at our fundraiser in Vegas."

I've never attended a fundraiser with him, but that's not really the point.

"A Navy SEAL." He grins, and it doesn't reach his eye. "I like what you guys do. You go after the high-value targets. We could use you here. Do you want to be the new Secretary of Defense?"

He laughs. I laugh. It's a joke, but it's not funny. "Thank you, sir, but I like where I'm at right now."

"What brings you to the White House?"

"Having lunch with an old friend on the NSC." He doesn't register the acronym, so I spell it out. "National Security Council. I heard a rumor about the new intelligence report—unclassified, of course."

"Yes, right. The new report. Very serious."

"You're being briefed on it next."

"I'm looking forward to that." He pauses. Hook, line, sinker. "Do you want to sit in on that briefing?"

"I don't have the clearance, sir."

"Round here, I make the clearance rules."

That's not even remotely true. I grin. "Excellent."

———

The Lieutenant-Colonel gives me a murderous look as she tries in vain to explain the legal agreement between the Five Eyes Alliance to a Commander-in-Chief who does not give a shit and has realized, belatedly, that he does not want this intelligence briefing that he convinced his Chief of Staff he did actually want.

I see how I've made this difficult for her, but it is her job, after all.

"Sir, the United States is bound by the UKUSA Agreement. It's a joint—"

"I don't give a flying fuck what agreements my predecessors signed. I didn't agree to that, and it sounds like horseshit. You want me to believe that New Fucking Zealand and the frozen wasteland that is Canada have better intelligence than the United States of America? Why is this the first I'm hearing about this?"

"At the analyst level, our intelligence assessment concurs with their reports."

"But we do have our own, independent data? Anything at all, not provided by those socialist yahoos, to believe that American business giants should be charged in an international court?" The President shakes his head. "Not on my fucking watch. We don't allow Americans to be tried for war crimes, we certainly aren't going to allow them to be tried for financial crimes by countries who don't understand our way of life."

It's his stump speech, I realize. He's memorized these lines, and they happen to sort of fit this situation, but it's not actually engaging with the question at hand.

"I have said it before, and I will say it again. The United States of America is not under attack. We have the best military and intelligence communities in the world, the best ever, and we are all very safe. Right, guys? That's what I've said, and that's what the intelligence reports should say, too."

Because he genuinely believes that his fantasies of how the world works is slick analysis.

Jesus Fuck, I can't stand here silent a minute longer. "Excuse me," I interrupt. "Sir, if you don't listen to your intelligence officers, you will wake up very soon to a rude surprise. An international court level of surprise. You don't want that problem. You can act now and investigate Mack Evans, Amelia Dashford Reid, and Gerome Lively—"

"Two of those people are dead, and that's a real shame, I gotta tell you. I don't know what your beef is with Mack, but he's a good guy. I'm having lunch with him this afternoon, in fact." POTUS narrows his eyes at me. "Who let you in here, anyway?"

"You did, sir." The final three words I got to say in the Oval Office before being escorted off the property by the Secret Service.

[22]

MELINDA

THE WHOLE TIME Jason is gone on some Boy Scout attempt to save the world—which isn't going to work, but has to be tried first, I guess—Wilson and Cole are trying their level best to get information out of me.

The conversation shifts back and forth between grilling me as a suspicious person and drawing out my perspective as an ally against a common enemy.

As Wilson tries to figure out if Jason's half-brother is even in the country—because the last flight plan filed by his pilot has him currently in Geneva—I do another round of dodging questions from Cole. Not because I don't want to answer them, exactly, but they're the wrong questions to be asking in the first place.

"I can't tell you my sources," I repeat for the third time. "That doesn't help us, anyway. Read the text message again. *You aren't playing my game. So I'm changing the rules.* This was all a game to him. All of it. And he thinks he's the puppet master. We need to be focused on his next steps, and right now, we don't even know what led him to this point."

Cole shakes his head. "You do, though. You know more than us."

"I don't have proof. Just hunches. That's what stories are half the time, hunches that we sit on for a very long time, maybe too long, because we have ethical standards to maintain."

"Like protecting your sources."

"Like verifying what they say with at least one other independent source," I snap back.

"Are your hunches protected? Can we start there?"

I take a deep breath. "Where do I start? I've been watching Mack for years. I didn't like him when I was with the foreign service. Those guys I saw this morning? I'm not surprised he has mercenaries on speed dial. He's deeply, quietly invested in a couple of private armies."

"Why keep that from us, though? We all know some guys who have gone and done that. We've hired some of them to be bodyguards. It's not like we have any kind of reputation to maintain."

"Ah, but you do." This is hard to explain. "You're the good-bad guys. For every rumor about The Horus Group, every salacious bit of gossip about that one time you covered up a murder, that creates the illusion that this is as depraved as Washington gets."

"We're some kind of cover? This whole time?"

"Not exactly. Five years ago, you split from whatever

role he first envisioned for you. I don't think he saw that coming. But when it did, that distance protected him *from* you, didn't it?"

"He helped us."

"That resistance to seeing what is right in front of you is exactly why I can't reveal my sources. It's why stories need to be researched and documented way beyond hunches. And it's why I've had to live with awful truths for a long fucking time, truths that *if you would just believe me*, could have radically altered the path of history five years ago."

Cole's jaw flexes. "Try me."

I don't like doing this. "Five years ago you flew to Miami on Mack's jet."

A broken, wounded sound comes from his mouth. "No."

Cole's wife was kidnapped after they landed in Miami, by Gerome Lively. They rescued her, and Lively was arrested, but he got a sweetheart deal and it wasn't until my book came out that he faced significant charges for other crimes.

"He set Hailey up."

"Why?" Cole shakes his head. "No, don't answer that. I see what you're saying now. Nobody wants to see the monster right in front of them. Motherfucker. I'll kill him."

"I get it. I do. But that doesn't actually solve anything. You cut off one head, another pops up elsewhere. Because it's all connected. PRISM. Lively's abuse of girls. You think he's the only one?"

Cole's eyes are blazing as he turns back to Wilson. "Where the fuck is he?"

"Officially, he's in Geneva. Unofficially...I have no idea. But I've created some chaos in his network, and the New York Stock Exchange has suspended trading in his company, so wherever he is, he'll have to show himself soon for a call with investors."

The elevator pings, and we all pivot in that direction. My jacked-up pulse doesn't settle down when we see that it's Jason, either.

His face is grim. He glances at the screen on the boardroom wall. "Looking for Mack's whereabouts? I think he's in New York." He gives us the summary of how it went at the White House. "POTUS is going to the United Nations this afternoon. He says he's having lunch with Mack, who is a *good guy*." He laughs hollowly. "So whatever game Mack is playing, he's buying time to get past that lunch."

"Or killing time, maybe?" I swallow hard against that ugly thought. "Maybe he's bored. Maybe everything has already been set in motion, and he's playing with us like a cat plays with string."

"Either way, the president takes off in an hour. He has a plane at the ready, and we do not. How are we going to beat him to NYC?"

"Maybe we don't need to..." Wilson pops a world map up on the screen. "Ellie asked me some smart questions about secure air-gap networks yesterday. But I have a few new data points that reveal something interesting."

Two emails appear on the screen, one from Mack

Evans to Jason, which had been forwarded to Wilson, and the other a direct reply from Mack to Wilson after a follow-up question. "Jason, remember this query from Mack a year ago? He attached images to both emails, two days apart. Look at the image properties." The same four and a half minute time gap between creation and last opened. "These two emails were sent from different parts of the world. Ellie was asking me about how to hack into a secure network, air-gaped from the wider internet. But I think what we're looking at is the result of some sort of scrambling device or app that is hard-wired into Mack's life. On his phone, his computer, everywhere."

Of course he doesn't have the Lively documents spirited away in a fortress somewhere.

Mack Evans believes he *is* a fortress.

MELINDA

"He has power because he has secrets. Let's unmask him. If he inherited the stash of blackmail material from Lively, and he can access it wherever he his, then that means we can access it, too. Right?"

Wilson nods. "There's always a way in. Let's start with his private office here in D.C. How do we want to do this? His private military guys are going to be on high alert."

Cole shrugs. "We can handle them. He wants a game? We'll give him a game." He gives me a hard look. "Want to see a part of our offices you didn't know about five years ago?"

"Is it the secret armory behind your office?" I give them all my sweetest smile as they gape at me. "What? I'm very good at what I do. But I'd love to be better acquainted with it. If he has a private army, I want one, too."

That's not an understatement, either. They have bulletproof vests, high-tech comms equipment, and enough fire-power to start a war. Or end one.

Wilson has a mobile comms center as well, and once he's ready to go, we return to the parking garage. Jason leads us to a white Mercedes van. From the outside it looks like any other repair or service vehicle, but inside, it's a tank.

He holds out his hand, and I take the boost. I ignore the tremor of fear that whispers, *he said he doesn't trust you.* Yeah, well, he also said he loves me, and I'm putting all my faith in that.

Tag drives. Wilson gives me the world's fastest lesson in hacking. My job is pretty simple. I just need to connect a portable transponder into Mack's network. "The trick is that you don't know what options you will have until we get there. It might be a USB drive, it might need to be a Smart TV. Hell, it could be the fridge. Rich people are stupid and connect a lot of shit to the internet. But for this, we need to be prepared that it'll be trickier. So you've got a bunch of tools here..." He runs through them all. A tiny laptop that I can plug into the wall, which will search the electricity grid for wired network connections. A USB device with a radio transmitter, and a couple of different Bluetooth scanners with password decoders built in. Everything fits into a small black bag. "While you're doing that, Jason will be right in lock step with you. He's got your back. Cole will clear the rooms ahead of you. Got it?"

"Got it."

"At the first sign of overload, we call in the Feds. If there is shooting, you get down."

I nod.

"And if I can't gain remote access, you may need to send the files my way."

"Easier from the inside than the outside," I whisper.

"Exactly. You remember. Upload it in chunks," Wilson says. "That way if you're interrupted, we still have some of it."

"Got it."

"We're not going to be interrupted," Jason growls.

"Fingers crossed," I whisper.

"I'll kill the power in there, give you time to get inside. When the power comes back on, you won't have long before there's company."

"We'll be quick."

Tag pulls up in the alley behind Mack's office. We get out of the van. I keep my eyes locked on the little red light on the keypad on the door. The second it blinks out, and Cole pulls the door open, a countdown clock starts in my mind.

Jason holds me back as Cole clears the main floor, then we creep ahead. We scan the rooms on the main floor, but I don't see any obvious smart devices.

Cole radios from upstairs that the building is empty, and we take the stairs as fast as we can.

Jason leads the way to Mack's office, which is locked, but Cole makes short work of that with a picking kit. He clears it, then we head inside.

I search the desk area while Jason scans for bugs and cameras.

Bingo.

"There's an ethernet connection," I murmur into my headpiece. "Connecting the laptop now."

"Standing by to reconnect power."

Jason sprays black paint over a small camera in the ceiling. "Ready when you are."

The lights flicker back to life and the computer boots up. I watch as Wilson's remote access runs an override into the backend of the system.

"Okay, you're in. What are we looking for?"

We'd brainstormed a bunch of search words and key phrases, which he has bots looking for, but I'm also going to poke around manually.

Sometimes, nothing replaces good old human intelligence.

Or human stupidity. It takes me five clicks deep into a folder to find a virtual locked box. Might as well put a red flag on it. "Wilson, can you help unlock this for me?"

Ten seconds later, the folder opens. I recognize the file naming conventions from what was released during the Lively investigations. "This is it."

"Copy it in batches," Wilson reminds me. "Pick the stuff that's most valuable first."

It's all valuable. Every image is a young girl who had her innocence stolen. Every email is proof that could put someone away for a long time.

My heart pounds as I carefully select the first hundred files and copy to the USB drive, which sends it to Wilson.

"We have company," Wilson says. "Front entrance. Two guys."

Jason taps his radio in acknowledgment. Then he kisses me. "Stay here."

"You have to stop—" I cut myself off. "I'll stay here."

"This is where the good stuff is, anyway. You keep copying those files. I'll be right back."

I grab another hundred files. Then another.

I'm halfway through the folder when I hear a creak in the wall. Heart pounding, I select the rest and say a silent prayer as I drag it to the USB drive. Here's hoping they go through.

I shove the computer deep under the desk as a panel on the wall opens, and Mack Evans steps into the room.

He's armed, and furious.

He prowls in my direction, and not for the first time, I note the brotherly resemblance in the shape of their bodies, the way they hold their arms at their sides, the killer look in their eyes.

I much prefer Jason's killer stare, if I'm being honest. This one has zero charm and is actually homicidal.

"You're a nosy fucking bitch, aren't you? Couldn't let a dead man's secrets die with him."

"Nice to see you, too." I won't show him fear. I won't give him that thrill. "I thought you had a lunch date with a politician."

Mack sneers at me. "I'll be late for it, I guess. Got stuck in traffic. Don't have a motorcade...yet."

"How does this end?"

"It doesn't." He gives me a chilly smile. "Why would you think it ends here? You might end here, but *it*, the grand experiment, it never ends."

"You're delusional."

"You're naïve." His eyes flash. "This is fun. Is this what it's like with Jason? No wonder he can't resist you."

He's goading me. I won't raise to the bait. "You have a weird idea of fun. This... what did you call it? This game? You're playing it all by yourself."

"Hardly." He gestures the gun he's holding, indicating for me to move. "Come away from the desk. Slowly."

I shift my weight from one foot to the other. I can move as slow as molasses. I stop after a half-step in his direction. The files are still uploading, and I need to keep him talking.

"I heard a rumor that the UN is going to start an investigation into PRISM."

"It won't go anywhere."

"You're confident."

"I hold all the cards."

I wonder how many international leaders are implicated in the files I'm currently sending to Wilson. *Keep talking.* "Are they cards you got from Lively?"

"He was a fool. Obsessed with his craven desires. He lost focus on what really matters."

"And that is?"

"Making the world a better place."

"Is that what you think you are doing? Nobody elected you to this. Nobody wants you to do this. You are a single, solitary mad man."

"This is what my country needs."

"No, it's not. And the sad thing is, you are far from the first person to think that—you are not an original thinker in this regard," I spit out. Another half step, and I prop my hands on my hips. "We have played out this script many times before, and America always finds its way back to justice and dignity. Not perfectly. Not for everyone. But we're working on it. Others are working on it, fiercely and bravely, and you will not stop them. Not today, and not ever again."

"What do you think you're going to do? Kill me and it will stop? I've set it all in motion, little girl." His hand shakes as he spews venom at me. "Plus, I got to have my fun with your little friend Caroline. While you were distracting Jason with your sweet tits and wet pus—"

I pull my Sig from the holster on my back and pull the trigger in one fluid motion. "That's enough out of you," I say after he crumbles to the ground.

Jason bursts through the door. "Ellie!"

"I—"

"It's—" He stops, eyes wide, and stares at his brother lying on the floor. "Did you...?"

"He really deserved it," I say faintly.

He races around the desk and grabs my hand, but I don't move.

"He really deserved it," I repeat. The words hammer in

my skull right along with, *I killed your brother. Please forgive me.*

"Come on. We have to get out of here. There are more of those mercenaries coming."

"One more minute. It's still uploading."

"Ellie, leave it."

I stand up, reluctantly. I want every last bit of evidence.

There's a crack in the air, something sharp.

"Ellie!" His voice is sharp, urgent. Full of panic.

I turn slowly, the world around me disassociating from the sound of his voice and the sluggish pump of blood through my veins. *What*, I mean to ask. It doesn't come out. I make it as far as opening my mouth, and then everything goes black.

[24]

JASON

"Sniper!" I yell as I drop, desperate to get across to Ellie now. She's bleeding, a pool forming under her body, but I can't see where she was hit.

So much blood.

Outside, there is return fire. Sirens.

Inside, I'm a man clawing his way through slick red mess, trying to find a wound to put pressure on.

Boots on the stairs.

Voices in the distance. "He's not dangerous, don't shoot. *Medic.* We have two people down in here!"

They're wrong, though.

One person, one monster.

I stare down at Ellie's pale face. *No,* she would say. *He's a person, too. People are monsters every day.*

Two people down in here, and it's all my fault.

[25]

MELINDA

THE FIRST TIME I wake up, there are way too many
beeping machines and bright lights. I can't keep my eyes
open, and Jason's face swims in front of me for a hot second
before I drift again.

The second time, it's dark and quiet, and my throat is
dry. I try to use my voice and nothing comes out, so I just
blink up at the ceiling for a moment.

I'm in the hospital.

I'm alive.

My neck is stiff, but it works enough to look right—a
curtain, and a door past that. I'm in a regular room. A
private room.

I look left, and I realize I'm not alone. Jason is sleeping
in a chair in the corner. His hair is standing on end, he
hasn't shaven in what looks like days at least, if not a week.

But I smile, because I'm alive, and he's right there.

It hurts to kick my feet, and my arms are heavy, too, but I'm pretty sure I have control of my limbs.

Twisting sends a sharp burning pain up my side, though. Fuck. A gasp, and it comes out a rough croak.

Jason's eyes fly open. "Ellie," he says roughly, surging to his feet. He hits a button on the wall. "You're awake."

"Mmm." *I love you.* "Mm-urgh."

"Shhh. It's been a few days. Hang on, I'll get you some water."

I try to take a deep breath and make myself cough, which holy shit, really hurts. He comes around to the right and holds a lidded cup with a straw out for me to sip at.

"Little sips."

A nurse bustles in behind him, and the light flicks on. I groan and close my eyes. "Too bright."

"Hey, those are words!" Jason sounds down right thrilled at my basic ability to communicate.

"What...happened?"

"Later. I'll tell you later." His lips brush my temple. "I gotta get out of her way or she's going to kick me," he whispers. "I'm so glad you're awake."

The straw returns to my mouth, and a woman's voice, the nurse, instructs me to sip again. Then she tells me she needs to check my vitals and reflexes, and I crawl back inside my mind for a bit.

I think I was shot.

That's why my side hurts.

Why was I asleep for so long?

[26]

JASON

"Iт's normal for people to sleep a lot when they've gone through a trauma. Maintaining consciousness is hard work, especially when someone is in extreme pain. We've upped her dosage, but honestly, rest is best right now. You should go home and get some yourself."

I nod as the surgical resident gives me the spiel after checking in. It's been an hour since Ellie woke up briefly, and she's fast asleep again.

Her color is a thousand times better than it was, though. Her cheeks have pinked up. It may be wishful thinking, but I swear her chest is rising and falling with greater range, too. I'm not a doctor, but I really think she's doing just fine now.

I'll go home when I can take her with me.

A knock at the door makes me jump. The nurses and doctors don't knock, and everyone else should be stopped by the U.S. Marshals, who have extended protection to Ellie while the FBI investigation takes place.

But the visitor has a badge, too.

Kendra Browning steps inside the room. "How's the patient doing?"

"Still unconscious." I don't tell her that Ellie woke up briefly. It's irrelevant.

"I just wanted to let you know that our tussle over the shooting's jurisdiction has ended. The FBI is taking the rest of the investigation, but the homicide investigation officially belongs to MPDC."

"It wasn't a homicide," I point out.

"A man is dead."

"And a woman is fighting for her life because of one of his employees."

Kendra nods. "You don't have to convince me. But it's not my case. Conflict of interest."

"Because of Tag?"

She shakes her head. "I met with Melinda a few days before the shooting. I was following a rumor. Photos from Gerome Lively's plane. Do you know anything about that?"

My bones ache with exhaustion. I can't believe that a week ago, I thought I was getting too old for the spy game. A week ago, I had no fucking idea what old felt like. "Yeah," I mutter. "I know something about that."

"There are a lot of people who want to bury that evidence," Kendra murmurs. "I'm not one of those people."

"You and Ellie have that in common."

"And you?"

I don't know where I stand on anything anymore. "I just want her to wake up."

"That's understandable. When she does, tell her I'm eager to talk to her."

I nod. "Will do."

When the door closes, I move my chair closer to the bed and lean forward, pressing my head against Ellie's hip. After a minute, her hand moves, brushing against my cheek.

I whisper her name.

"Hi," she whispers back.

Turning my head, I look at her. "You're awake again."

"I heard some of that." Her voice catches, and I sit up so I can pass her the water cup. She sips, then sighs. "Am I in trouble?"

"No."

"Thought it was a good sign I wasn't in handcuffs." She tries to smile.

"I wouldn't let them."

"Did they try?"

"No." I look at the door. "There are Marshals out there. You're safe. You're being protected."

"From who?" Her brow furrows. "Oh right. Cut off one head..."

"The full force of the FBI is on this right now. Don't worry about it."

She licks her lips. "Dry."

"More water."

A nod. "And lip balm?"

I smile. "I don't have any."

"My backpack…"

"I'll get you some."

"I want my backpack."

"Okay." I smooth my hand over her forehead. "Keep resting."

She tries to lift her hand, but it doesn't go far. I reach for her fingers and gently lace them through mine. "I was dreaming about you."

"Good. Do more of that."

A smile drifts across her face. "Okay."

[27]

MELINDA

THE NEXT TIME I wake up, I stay up for an hour. Wilson shows up, insisting that Jason needs a shower and some rack time in his own bed. I agree.

"I'm not going anywhere, and I've got good company."

Wilson waves an iPad in the air. "I brought movies." His other hand hoists a bag of yarn in the air. "And crafts, too."

"You still knit?"

"Sometimes. It's a good way to pass the time on planes."

"Are you going home soon?"

"I've been there and come back again. I'll return at the end of the week, probably. Then you won't see me for a good long while."

Jason gives me a searching look. I avoid his gaze. I don't know how to deal with the unspoken question. Will I see any of them? Do I even want to?

This isn't a conversation to have in front of Wilson. "Can you knit me socks?"

"After you saved the world? It's the least I could do."

Jason frowns. "Are your feet cold? Do you want me to get you a warm blanket before I go?"

I wiggle my fingers at him. "I'll be fine."

He leans in and brushes his lips against mine.

I wrinkle my nose. "You could bring me a toothbrush and toothpaste. And my backpack!"

"I remember."

"Thank you."

"I'll be back soon."

Predictably, I fall asleep before he returns, but when I wake up, I'm rewarded with a freshly shaved and showered, very handsome man sitting beside me. He's reading a book, some non-fiction modern philosophy title.

My feet feel warm. "I have socks on?"

Jason jerks his head up. "Yep. Wilson...well, apparently he was already working on a pair for his partner, who was happy to donate them to the Ellie's-Cold-Toes good cause."

I wiggle my no-longer-cold-toes. "Can you lift the blanket so I can see them?"

He carefully reveals my feet, wrapped in bright red socks with purple toes.

I gasp. "I love them!"

He grins. "Good."

My stomach growls. "Do you think I'm allowed to eat anything?"

The nurse allows me some Jello, so while I nibble on that, I ask Jason to catch me up on the latest.

"Actually, the socks are related to the most recent news."

"How so?"

"Did you follow the Spencer Rook story before the election?"

I frown. "Yes. He was a white nationalist. He was shot in a showdown with the FBI."

Jason shook his head. "Wilson shot him. It's a long story, but it was deeply personal."

"Oh. Wow."

Jason takes a deep breath. "One of the things the FBI has uncovered is a financial connection between Mack and Spencer Rook. My brother hosted Rook and some of his fascist friends for private dinner parties, over quite a long period of time. He gave them seed money, too."

I don't know what to say to that. "I'm so sorry."

"Yeah. Well, Wilson is extra grateful for you putting an end to another neo-nazi."

I push the Jello aside. "Jason..."

"I'm fine."

"How can you be fine? He was your brother, and I..."

He takes my hand and looks at me, his expression fierce. "When I say I'm fine, I mean, I will be fine. I mean, I'm so fucking grateful that you survived. I mean, I'm gutted that I didn't see it earlier. And I don't know if I could have pulled the trigger, but I hope I could have.

That's what I mean. I'm fine. I'm far from good, but I could be so much worse."

I nod.

"Finish your Jello."

I've lost my appetite, though.

———

The next morning, my catheter comes out, and I'm allowed to shower all by myself. I come out of the bathroom dressed in real clothes, feeling like a million bucks.

And then the day gets even better. Deacon Webb appears at the door. "You have a visitor."

The gasp I let out when Caroline walks in the door is almost embarrassing. Almost, but not at all. "I'm so happy to see you," I whisper as she gently squeezes me. "I have something for you."

She hands me a stuffed bear from the gift shop. "That was supposed to be my line."

I laugh, which hurts, but it's worth it. "I, uh, found your condoms. At the gym?"

"Oh. Those." Her eyes go wide with meaning. "Okay."

"I didn't...use them. Open them." She giggles and I hold my side. "No funnies. Whatever is inside, I haven't seen it. They're in my backpack over there."

She gives me another wide-eyed look and digs them out. "Oh, look at what I found just sitting in plain sight."

"I figured, a room being guarded by U.S. Marshals is pretty safe."

Laughing, she nods, then joins me on the bed. "You could have looked."

"I didn't need to. We sorted it out."

"Better than we had," she confesses. "The files named Mack Evans as a person of interest, but nothing like what you figured out."

"Speaking of that..." I take a deep breath. "Wilson has a giant cache of documents. He hasn't looked at them. We, uh, didn't exactly tell the FBI about them."

Caroline's head looks like it might actually explode. "Mel!"

"Yeah, I know. But that wasn't my call, because I was in an ambulance, and the Horus Group...it's not in their nature to be forthcoming with law enforcement."

"Men."

"I hear you. So I need a federal prosecutor I can trust to turn the bulk of the documents over to. Even redacted, I think they reveal too much about the girls who were abused. It would be better if investigators could quietly search those girls out and get their permission before the documents are released."

"No more burning it all to the ground?"

"I'll find a way to do that without using those images. It's enough that we have them. They shouldn't be made public."

"I'll help you."

"I don't know if it's your jurisdiction..."

"We'll find a way to make sure it is. There were certainly enough dead bodies in my jurisdiction."

"I'm only responsible for one of them."

"In self-defense," she adds. "You're responsible for one of them in self-defense."

Sure. That's sort of true on a cosmic level.

———

The next day, I'm discharged, and the Marshals clear me to stay with Jason. He takes me back to his place, which is palatial compared to my apartment in Georgetown, but just as Spartan.

"As you can see, I never got around to decorating."

"We have that in common."

"On the upside, there's lots of room for your stuff." Jason smiles awkwardly. "If you're willing to move in here while you recuperate."

"I..." I let out a shaky laugh. "Yeah. I'm willing."

"I wasn't sure."

The space between right now and when I might be able to get on a plane and go home to California seems both infinite and minute at the same time. "We haven't had much privacy to talk about...everything."

"I don't want to rush you."

"I love you." They come out in such a rush, they sound like a single word. "I know it's very complicated, and we have spent more time not trusting each other than actually being honest, but deep down and through it all, I have found my way back to you over and over again. I'm messy, Jason. Messy and carrying a lot of baggage. I, unlike you, am not fine. Not at all. But when you told me that you loved me, that gave me all the strength I needed. And I just wanted to say it back. No strings attached."

"No strings?"

I shake my head. "I don't expect anything in return."

"Okay." He shrugs. "Sounds good."

Then he walks out of the living room.

My mouth falls open. "Jason!"

He comes back. "Yeah?"

"I lied. Maybe. I do expect *something* in return for that. Like...I dunno."

"Do you want to talk more about moving in here?"

I live in California. "Sure." I swallow hard. "I may not have a lot of stuff, but I do have an aloe vera plant named Monica. She needs a window seat. That's important."

He nods. "I like Monica. We can make sure she has a place of honor."

"You like her?"

"I like her very much. She reminds me of you."

"Prickly?"

"Prickly on the outside. Wet and juicy on the—" He cuts himself off and closes the gap between us. "No?" He howls as I shove him gently. "I mean, slippery and sweet—" Another shove, although I have zero strength right now. "How about beautifully slick and unexpectedly healing on the inside?"

"We can accept that." But I'm secretly happy that he's making wet pussy jokes. That has to be a sign that he's getting over his guilt at seeing me shot, and back to seeing me as a desirable woman. "Do you want to show me the rest of the apartment?"

"Yeah." He takes my hand and guides me through the kitchen, then down a hallway. There's an office first, and a workout room across from it, and at the end, a door to a large master bedroom.

In the window is my aloe vera plant, and she looks very happy.

[28]

JASON

I'M SO FUCKING nervous as Ellie stands in my bedroom, looking at her plant. Not saying anything.

I would do anything to make this moment better for her. To be a regular man who could have wined and dined her, a man who took her to dinner after work a few times a week, and cooked with her the rest of the time.

A regular Joe.

That's what she deserves.

"I have food," I blurt out. "So I can cook something for you."

She nods. "I'm not really hungry."

I need to be so careful with her. She's still healing. Still needs her rest.

"Do you want to lie down?" That gets me another nod. "We can talk more about you staying here. I shouldn't have made a joke before. I just thought it was funny that you brought up the plant, and I'd already grabbed it."

"Her."

I smile. "Her. There's no rush to talk about what comes next."

She gives me a curious look, then slowly unbuttons her blouse. "Okay."

It's hypnotic. Her little fingers, the bare flashes of flesh as the fabric slides open. I shouldn't be this easily turned on, not when she's—

"Jason?"

"Mmm." She's not wearing anything under the blouse. Her breasts pebble under my gaze, her nipples pulling tight.

"I don't really want to talk about the future." She peels off her jeans, and stands in front of me in a skimpy pair of cotton panties—and a bandage on her side. "I want to have sex."

I groan deep in my throat. "Sex."

"It's better than talking." She reaches for me, her fingers sliding under my shirt and over the taut, warm skin of my belly. My muscles clench against her arousing touch.

"I shouldn't— We shouldn't—"

"Yes, we should," she whispers as I lift her ever so gently and lie her on the bed.

I kiss her mouth. "I was so scared I'd lose you." I kiss her jaw. Her neck. I rake my mouth over the fragile skin on her chest. But I can't move any lower. I can't look at that bandage. "I can't hurt you now."

"Gently, then." She arches beneath me.

"Stop moving so much. You'll rip a stitch."

"I'm pretty healed up already." But then she winces.

"Hold still," I rasp. "Hold absolutely fucking still, and I will make you feel good."

A nervous, ugly fear twists inside me as I ease her panties down her legs. But then she slides her thighs apart, revealing that pink sweetness I am intoxicated, and the fear gets good and tangled with need.

Gently, I settle in beside her, on the opposite side from her stitches. She has bruises all over her belly, too. But between her legs, she's warm and swollen, just slippery enough for me to slick up her clit with her own arousal.

"I love you," she whispers as I stroke her soft pussy lips. Up and down, then in just a little.

"I love you, too." Up and down, then a little deeper this time. It takes an agonizingly long time for me to sink my whole finger into her, she's impossibly tight, and there's no way I'm fucking her until we get a clean bill of health for physical activities.

It's enough to just touch her, though. I stroke her slowly, endlessly, as if she's a precious china doll, and she does exactly as I ask. She holds perfectly still, even as her hunger to climax grows. Even as she begs me to go faster, and I don't, but I ramp up the pressure on her clit, and then, just as she nears the peak, I add a second finger.

My name rips from her lips, then a gasp, her face contorting. I worry I've hurt her, but then a blissful expression slides into place.

"I needed that." She rubs her cheek against the pillow. "Oh yes, I really did."

Maybe I did, too. I pull the blanket over her and we curl up together, finally at peace.

[29]

MELINDA

IT TAKES A SHOCKINGLY long time to get my strength back. Weeks slide into a month, then suddenly, two months is around the corner.

I've started writing again, but the breaking news I had been working on was broken by other people, while I was unconscious, and then recovering. That's life, and I don't need to chase stories at all if I don't want to.

But I do want to, that's the problem.

I know I should talk to someone about that—Caroline, maybe. Jason, almost certainly. A therapist, no doubt. But I don't do any of that. Instead, I think on it, stewing, and suddenly two months have gone by and I realize—shit, I'm grumpy.

"I was thinking," Jason says one morning after we shower together, and he is painfully gentle with me, as always. "How would you feel about going out for dinner?"

I burst into tears.

He stares at me in horror. I stare right back, equally horrified, because I don't cry, and if I did, it wouldn't be over a very reasonable suggestion that it is maybe time to return to the land of the living.

"No, it's too soon," he corrects, albeit wrongly.

"It's not too soon," I say, furiously wiping my eyes. "It's that I want more for my life than dinner to be a momentous event." I take a really deep, all the way to the bottom of my lungs breath. "I don't have any good stories to write, and I'm worried I won't ever again, and I'm feeling a bit cooped up."

He nods. "Okay. Yep. That's bad. Let's fix that."

I slump against him. "Can we fix it over dinner?"

So he makes a reservation at a very private restaurant in Arlington, and I get dressed up. It's the first time since the shooting that I've put on makeup—and the first time since I left California that I'm staring at myself in the mirror as I do so, and not some carefully constructed alter-ego.

Jason comes in as I put the finishing touches. He stands behind me and brushes my hair, now long enough to cover my shoulders, out of the way so he can kiss my neck.

"You look good enough to eat," he whispers.

I shiver at the tempting thought. "Yes, please."

"Right here?" He spins me around and lifts me onto the bathroom counter. "Hold on tight."

I lean back against the mirror, bracing my hands on the counter, and he kneels in front of me. "You look good, too." I let out a breathy laugh as he nips the inside of my thigh.

Ever so slowly, he's getting rougher and more intense with me. I grab on to each moment with both hands.

He tugs my panties to the side and kisses my sex, a soft open-mouthed taste that ends in a teasing flick of his tongue against my clit. I rock against his face, suddenly very horny, but he only gives me two more slow-tongued kisses there before he stands up and crowds against me. "We'll be late for dinner."

"So mean," I breathe. Then I lunge at him, tasting myself on his lips.

He slams me back against the mirror, his hands cushioning behind me, and thrusts his tongue deep into my mouth. "Make no mistake," he growls. "I want more of that as soon as we get home. But we're going to go out for dinner, like grown-ups, and talk about grown-up things like work. And fucking."

I can't wait. I shimmy my hips and he helps me down again.

Then he looks at me again. "Something is different about your face."

I touch my bare mouth. He drops his gaze to my lips and smiles. "Yeah. You aren't wearing any lipstick."

I wrinkle my nose. "I don't, actually. Usually."

"Huh." He leans against the door frame. "You know, I wondered that. If the red and pink lipsticks were different personalities."

I groan. "Is that what we're calling my former identities?"

"Am I wrong."

"No." I give him an impish smile. "But yeah, this is the real me, I guess."

He takes my face in his hands and looks at me, really looks carefully. His gaze rakes over my mouth, my cheeks, and my heavily lined eyes. "Were you a goth as a kid by any chance?"

"Guilty as charged. I never really outgrew it."

"Fascinating. And yet when you were being someone else, you went ultra-feminine. I like both looks," he hastens to add. "I like *you*, and however you choose to decorate your face."

"A-plus answer."

Dinner is incredible. We take our time with each course, and as promised, we talk about work.

"It's actually amazing that nobody else has the details on the full scope of those incriminating images and emails. I'm still the only journalist who has the numbers, and most of the names." I drag in a deep breath. "For a long time, I thought if I got my hands on them, I'm dump them into the public like the Panama Papers. I even had a good name picked out for the release."

He waits expectantly.

"The Pervert Papers."

It gets a laugh. That makes me feel good. But then he shakes his head. "But you can't."

Nope. "I know. And I don't want to anymore, either. It's just, that's what I thought the scoop would be. So now it feels like dry procedural stories, which isn't what I do."

"No, it's not."

"If I can make a suggestion," he offers.

"Please."

"Go back to your roots. Only one of us managed to get Gerome Lively facing life sentences, and it wasn't me with my shock and awe takedown of him at sea. You did it by making individual narratives more powerful than anything else. I didn't know it was you, Ellie, but I was reading Melinda Gray from day one. You're very good at what you do."

My chest feels tight. I rub it. "What I do isn't enough, though."

"It is. And it will be again."

"I'm scared of letting those women down, letting down the girls they once were."

"Nobody is promised justice in this world, but that doesn't mean we don't keep trying to make it happen. That's all they expect from a superhero."

I sigh.

"Maybe that didn't help."

"No, it did." I take his hand across the table. "I didn't realize how sad I was about that."

"You compartmentalize a lot."

I snort. "Yeah."

We sit with that depressing thought for a few moments

in silence, then he leans in, just as I take a sip of water. "Which brings me to the grown-up discussion about fucking," he whispers.

I sputter, and water goes *everywhere*. "Jesus, I'm glad that wasn't wine."

"I need to work on my segues," he says innocently.

Except that was very deliberate.

My lover is a funny, funny man. "So, fucking, huh? What exactly about my locked-down emotional state would make you want to talk about—oh, I see what you did there."

"I think we both, because of who we are and how we have lived our lives, compartmentalize sex and intimacy."

"Fair point."

"And I've been thinking about that summer, five years ago." His gaze heats up, hungry and aroused.

"I think of it often," I murmur.

"Why was it so hot, and left such a lasting impression on us, if we weren't really being true to ourselves or each other?"

I think he's been reading just the right amount of modern philosophy books. "I have no idea, but I can't wait to hear your hypothesis."

He grins. "That summer—because it wasn't you, because *you knew* we could never amount to anything, and you knew you wouldn't be using me for a story—you were free to *role play* the combination of the two together. Sex plus intimacy."

"That's quite the hypothesis."

"You can tell me I'm wrong."

I shake my head. "You're not wrong. I think that's probably exactly right." I take a deep breath. "But I think we should finish the rest of this conversation at home."

———

Our drive back to his apartment is fraught with a delicious kind of tension. Inside, we open a bottle of wine and put on music, then fall onto the couch together.

"This was exactly what I needed," I murmur as he trails his fingers down my arm.

"We both needed it." He holds my gaze, but doesn't push.

We both know I've left some things unsaid, and now is the time to dig deeper. I reach out and touch his face. He's started to go gray, just a little, in all the right places.

Five years is a long time.

But I remember that summer so clearly. So I take a deep breath, and bare my soul. "It was so hard to see you again, after all that time. Scary. Absolutely frightening, and for no good reason that I could sort out. It took me a long time to admit to myself that it was so hard for me to be back in close proximity to you, because I knew that this time, I would have to know better than to fall in love with you."

His blue eyes narrow, piercing me with their intensity. "This time?"

I'm shaking. "I'd already fallen for you once. I fell in love with you five years ago."

He's a statue, frozen and expressionless.

I run my fingers over his cheek and bravely push on. "I already walked away once, too, and I knew how hard that was. I couldn't let myself *feel* that deeply again. So I couldn't be the same person. I think I had to hold part of myself back."

He catches my wrist, stilling my fingers. Then he slowly turns his head and kisses the inside of my forearm, raising goosebumps. "And now? Are you still holding something back?"

I shake my head slowly. "But it's taken me a while to get my strength back, and I think *you* are maybe holding something back."

He looks genuinely surprised. "Me?"

"You don't need to be gentle with me anymore."

"I want to be."

"I know. But I want...the full range of experiences. Gentle. Hard. Demanding. Bossy. Needy. Urgent—"

He puts both of his hands on my waist and hauls me into his lap. Hard, demanding, and very urgent. "So we both need to let go of worry."

"Yes," I whisper. My breath is a prayer. How lucky am I? It's an absolute miracle that I get to show him how much I love him and how much I want him. But I don't say anything else.

He traces my jaw with his fingertips, then taps my lower lip. "Spread your legs for me."

I twist in his lap so I'm straddling him.

He teases his fingertips along the elastic of my underwear. "Tell me what you want next."

I squirm against his erection. "I want to ride you like this. I want you to pull my panties to the side and tell me..." I shiver. "Tell me to put your cock into my tight little pussy."

"Jesus, I've missed your dirty mouth." He kisses me hard, then tugs my underwear to the side exactly as I asked. "Do you want my cock?"

"Mm-hmm."

"I want to see your hands on it first. Unzip me."

I fumble at his zipper, so excited, and when I curve my hand into his pants, I find him dripping with pre-come for me. *Yes.*

"Jerk me," he whispers. "See that slippery seed? See how slick I am for you? I'm going to slide right into your body, all the way. That's how excited you've made with your perfect, filthy words. Understand?"

"Yes," I breathe.

"Rub your cunt against my cock. Show me that you're wet enough."

I roll my hips, desperate to bring us together. With his free hand, he squeezes the back of my neck. "Oh, that feels so good. I could come like this, use your soft little pussy to jack off."

I whimper. "Please."

"Please what?"

"I want to ride you. I want your cock inside me."

"Then put me inside you," he growls. "Show me that your tight pussy can take all of me."

I push up on my knees and rock forward, hurrying

because I'm aching for it now. I need that push, that stretch, that huge monster cock of his to fill me all the way up.

As soon as I find my hole, he pushes me down, his hand firm on my neck, me just a little itty bit of nothing in his arms, just a small sweet ball of sex on his lap, and I cry out because he fills me *more* than all the way up, he gets rid of that hollow feeling and then some.

"What's my name?" he growls.

I smile. "Jason."

"Who's deep inside you?"

"Jason."

"You can't hide from me. You can't hide that you need me."

I shake my head. *No*.

His eyes soften, just for a second. "And you don't need to, either."

I clamp my hands on his shoulders and start to ride him, start to find a rhythm, and his hands move to my ass, my hips, and then up my body, clawing at my dress to get my neckline down.

His mouth finds my tits, my nipples, making them all puffy and achy, and then, as my climax rumbles in hard and fast, like a storm on the ocean, his mouth finds my neck and latches on.

I come on his cock, as he spills deep inside me, and he gives me a hickey.

"That's it," he murmurs into my skin. "There. Gah, you're so good to me."

That really feels like something I should say to him, but I'm absolutely, completely wrung out.

[EPILOGUE]
MELINDA

JANUARY, TWO YEARS LATER

I's been a long time since I last stepped foot on the Langley campus. This time, I'm a civilian contractor with a unique security clearance granted by the newly sworn-in forty-sixth POTUS.

I'm here to teach a class to the newest batch of recruits. *Life on the Other Side* was the working title I joked about with Caroline and Wilson, who both gave me valuable feedback as I developed the lecture.

But it was Jason who helped me the most. Like so many of these trainees, he was indoctrinated in a selflessness instilled through military service, and that unwavering loyalty to his country was almost his downfall.

It was also what saved him in the end.

So the second working title was *Life on the Other Side*

of Unchecked Loyalty, but I know the game. That has to be the subtle takeaway, not the headline.

I turn my attention to the instructor, who is introducing me.

"It's my great honor to introduce Melinda Boyko, a former CIA operative who went on to have a remarkable second career in journalism under the anonymous pen name, Melinda Gray. She is the author of two bestselling non-fiction books, *Private Plane, Private Hell* and *The Undoing of Giants*. Today Ms. Boyko lives in California with her partner, and tries to visit Washington as little as possible." He looks up. "It says that in the bio, and I was instructed to read the entire thing without revision." The room erupts in laughter, which was my goal. Excellent. He smiles. "So it is obviously a great honor that she has agreed to spend the afternoon with us and present her lecture, *At the End of the Day, We're All Human*."

"Thank you so much," I say, stepping to the lectern. "And I'll be honest, I really wanted to give this as a TEDTalk, but I couldn't get the best parts de-classified." Another laugh. "Actually, the truth is there is no way that I could condense this talk into twenty minutes. Or do it without notes.

"My journey to this spot really begins not with my first day as a trainee, not with my time sitting where you are sitting right now, but with the day I handed in my resigna-tion. Today, I'm going to talk to you all about the fact that one day you won't be spooks any longer, and that's going to be...strange. There will be secrets you need to keep forever. From loved ones at first, but then as time goes on, even from yourself. You will compartmentalize what you once were in order to move forward and be something else. Something whole and vulnerable and very human. That is, if you're lucky. So let's dig into all the reasons why that might be hard, and how you can be the best spy possible for your government while also investing in your future self so you can have a long and healthy retirement as a barista in Kansas."

———

Jason is waiting for me when I finish. "I got the tour. Saw the chunk of the Berlin Wall, went to Stealth Starbucks."

"Was it everything you thought it would be and more?"

"Don't tease. Some of us didn't get to actually be spies."

"You're my spy."

"An excellent consolation prize." He kisses me warmly on the mouth. "Ready to head home?"

"Yep."

He takes me by the hand and leads me to the SUV we rented at the airport. We're not lingering here. Back on a flight tonight, and we'll land at LAX just as the sun sets. I didn't just include that line in my biography because it got a good laugh. It's the truth. Washington will forever be twisted up in trauma and misguided good intentions.

Particularly when waiting for us on the west coast is the crashing ocean, that magnificent breeze, and a quiet home perched high on top of a cliff.

The first thing Jason does when we arrive home is check to see if Monica needs a bit of water.

The second thing he does is pick me up and carry me to our bed.

"I have a new fantasy," I whisper as he sucks on my nipples through my shirt.

"Tell me."

"You're Batman. You catch me breaking into your Batcave and things get wild."

"Oh yeah?"

"Messy. Needy."

He groans.

Sex with Jason was, once upon a time, a game between two confidence artists.

We're just broken enough to admin that was good.

This is so much better.

"You get so mad at me. But then you want me, too, and there's some fumbling, too. Fingers would shake. And suddenly I'd be naked."

"I'd strip you down?"

"Mm hmm. And force me to my knees. You'd jerk off all over me."

He bites my neck and slides his hand into my pants at the same time. He finds me soaked.

"Can we do that now?" I gasp as he pinches my clit between two fingers. "I want to see you come. I want to watch your cock get even bigger. I want to see it throb, all dark and *full* like that. Your balls are aching, and I know you'd rather be between my legs."

"Fucking little tease," he growls. "Come here. You're getting fucked tonight. Your filthy blowjob fantasies will have to wait."

I scramble away from him, but he catches my ankle and hauls me down the bed as I giggle, out of control with love and lust for this man.

"I'm so happy," I whisper as he pins me down. "You make me so happy."

"I make you come."

"That's a big part of it," I say, mock-solemnly.

But the biggest part is that he moved across the country with me. He walked away from everything he had built and started over again out here, for me. I never would have asked him to do that. I was prepared to go back and forth. Tell him all my filthy superhero fantasies over the phone when we had to be apart.

But he didn't want that. He wanted to be right here, burying himself deep inside me at every opportunity.

"Are you absolutely going to lose it?" I pant. "Yes, Jason. Pin me down and fucking nut inside me. You're going to have to put your hand on my mouth, because I'm going to scream. I'm—"

He does as I ask and muffles me. I shudder in response.

My nipples ache from his mouth, a good ache, and between my legs, my slit is sloppy with need. This is everything. This is so hot and perfect. Jason holding me down, the heavy weight of him, his cock bare inside me.

Come inside me.

Mark me.

Make me whole.

And he does.

It takes us both a while to recover.

Jason's the first one to talk after we sprawl out. "Wow."

"Maybe one day you'll take me to your bat cave and we can do that for real."

He laughs. "Your mouth gets filthier every time, I swear. *Fucking nut inside you?*"

"That's when you started to come, wasn't it?"

"Damn straight."

"Do you think I could ever come out with something that's just right across the line?"

He laughs. "No, my beautiful little spy. Never."

"Why not?"

He grins. "Because I love your wild mind. I love the way it works, the stories it spins, and none of it scares me."

Who would have thought that a career as a spy and a sleuth would pay off one day in my love life like this.

Once a liar, always a liar.

I just use my powers for good now.

———

———

If you haven't read the other books in this series, you're in for a wild ride. Start with Cole and Hailey's story, Hate F*@k. (Seriously get on that, because you need Cole's dirty mouth in your life!)

The Forbidden Bodyguards Series

Hate F*@k (Cole and Hailey)
Booty Call (Ali and Scott)
Dirty Love (Wilson and Tabitha)
Wicked Sin (Taylor and Luke)
Filthy Liar (Jason and Melinda)

And if you're ready for more dirty romances, the first book in a new duet, TEMPT, is coming soon. Newsletter subscribers can read an exclusive prequel story for Sam and Hazel right now! Sign up on my website.

www.ainsleybooth.com

ACKNOWLEDGMENTS

This was such a hard book to write, and yet, I'm sad to be done with the Horus Group and this series. So much has changed since 2014 when I started writing Cole's book. I write to escape, and to provide escape, and I worried immensely that this series can't provide that anymore. But when I got Ellie and Jason alone together in a room, they were a lot of fun. I hope that came across.

For a million reasons, I want to leave this book on a simple note of thanks to my readers. You have changed my life, and I can't wait to share future stories with you. Thank you for putting your trust in me.

~ Ainsley

www.ainsleybooth.com